Elisabetta Sangalli

LEONARDO DA VINCI

and the Twelve Stones of Heaven

genialtutor.com

1. Il *Cenacolo* di Leonardo dopo l'ultimo restauro (1999)
   Milano, refettorio di Santa Maria delle Grazie
   The *Last Supper* of Leonardo after the last restoring (1999)

2. Part. degli apostoli a destra del Cristo. *The apostles on the right of Christ*

Edition and Copyright

Publisher, Editing, texts and graphics, ebook programming:

Dott. Ing. Tiziano Radice

Text correction and page layout:

Tiziano Radice ed Elisabetta Sangalli

First edition: November 1st, 2016

Second edition: March 3rd, 2019

Copyrights 2016: genialtutor.com

Much thanks to:

Mrs. Helen Valentine and Mrs. Jennifer Camilleri for the kind supplying of the image from the Royal Academy of Arts.

Mrs. Marylin Evans of Magdalen College of Oxford for the information about the Last Supper of Giampietrino.

Father Ivo Cleiren of the Abbey of Tongerlo, for the kind supplying of images with copyright of Thill NV, Brussels.

Herr Manfred Zips (Congregation of Minorite of Vienna), for the photographic material sent to me about the mosaic of Giacomo Raffaelli.

Mrs. Sarah Harel Hoshen, Curator of Judaica in the Jewish Museum in London, for information about the current version of the hòshen.

Madame Anne Giroux of the Musée du Louvre concierge service, for reporting on the research material.

C. Gamberini, E. Gasco, M. Vallarino (Episcopal Seminary of Savona).

Finally, a heartfelt thanks to prof. Giovanni Paolo Maggioni for his support and valuable suggestions and supervision of the text.

Presentation

Following the publication of Elisabetta Sangalli's interesting study has been a source of particular satisfaction to me. For the first time, a comprehensive text has seriously addressed the stone symbolism in Leonardo's Last Supper in Milan taking into account numerous factors starting with the Jewish tradition, continuing through the intense cultural climate in Lombardy at the end of the fifteenth century and encompassing Dominican customs, so rich in the theological considerations that provided Leonardo with his repertoire of precious stones.

Studying a painting conceived for monastic life means investigating its wealth of theological content: Leonardo's Last Supper is a one of a kind painting whose spiritual content marks it out and highlights the close relationship between Holy Scripture and religious life. It is a complex Eucharistic work, rich in a symbolism which derived as much from the Dominican fathers as the grand Master himself.

As the reader may therefore be stated, in addition to modern editorial presentation and the interesting scientific content, the advantage of this publication is the precious photographic documentation, proposed by the author in specific tables, allowing time to time a direct comparison between original work and copies, for a close and comprehensive reading of Leonardo's masterpiece and its details.

This text proposes a reinterpretation of Leonardo's master-piece by means of an analysis of its twelve precious stones. A depth of detail which may, at first sight appear meaningless, may actually be fundamental to our understanding of the work of art as details revealing underlying thought.

Publisher

Dott. Ing. Tiziano Radice

Introduction

Faced with a masterpiece of art such as Leonardo's Last Supper we inevitably feel a sense of loss. Writing about such a masterpiece means firstly accepting a difficult challenge because no painting in the world has been more copied, studied and admired.

This book, however, was born of a personal observation: preparing a presentation on Leonardo's masterpiece, and observing its fine details one day I focused my attention on the precious green stone that Leonardo painted on Christ's neck. It felt like I had never seen it before and yet it was not the first time that I had examined the painting; indeed, I knew the details of the stones but never, until that moment, I had wondered what they meant.

Yet, in painting the Last Supper, a great work 'whose every detail was finished' and with the addition of many descriptions, the artist left nothing to chance. Nor did he give free rein to his imagination with no meaning attached. Why then did he paint these stones and where did he source his iconography? What message was he trying to communicate and on what basis did he choose his stones when he chose to associate them with the apostles and the Divine Master?

My journey in discovery of the mystery of the twelve stones began here. I chose to take a new approach, to examine this unexplored iconography and its underlying spirituality, to bring out a novel Leonardo, a secret side to be examined and studied and one that may bring us the thrill of new discovery.

Author

Elisabetta Sangalli

November 1st, 2016, All Saints' Day

I delight greatly in the Lord; my soul rejoices in my God. For he has clothed me with garments of salvation and arrayed me in a robe of his righteousness, as a bridegroom adorns his head like a priest, and as a bride adorns herself with her jewels. (Isaiah 61, 10)

3. Part. della figura di Cristo al centro della scena. *Christ at the center of the scene.*

4. Part. degli apostoli a sinistra del Cristo. *The apostles on the left of Jesus.*

Leonardo's Last Supper

Leonardo came to Milan in 1482, summoned there by Ludovico il Moro's Sforza court as the duke's engineer. At that time Milan offered an unusual cultural background open to scientific study and technological progress and Leonardo proved unable to resist its call.

The artist *par excellence*, in 1495 he began work on his *Last Supper* at Milan's Santa Maria delle Grazie monastery, soon to become sole object of his studies and a project that he was to conclude only in early 1498[1]. As is well-known, the painting illustrates Christ's farewell supper with his friends and, in particular, the exact moment when the Saviour announces his betrayal at the hands of one of his close friends and evangelist Matthew narrates: 'Truly, I say to you, one of you will betray me'[2], which unleashes the most diverse reactions, specific to each apostle.

Obsessed with perfection, Leonardo chose to paint the scene using an insubstantial technique - tempera made from linseed oil and egg on a double layer of plaster - which unlike traditional fresco painting allowed him second thoughts, additions and nuances just like an oil painting. His choice of painting method, its north facing position and continual changes in temperature (the wall the painting is on separated the kitchen from the monastery's dining hall), the frequent and sometimes brutal restoration work the painting was subjected to in the following centuries in an attempt to curb the unstoppable degradation and finally aerial bombardment during the Second World War (in August 1943 the refectory vault was destroyed[3] resulted in the loss of many details of the work. This is the case of the gems painted on the clothing of the apostles and Christ only some of which are still visible today.

Investigating the stones Leonardo painted in the *Last Supper* and understanding their mysterious meaning requires starting long ago, going back in time, understanding both the internal Sforza milieu which the artist found himself directly working in, and another cultural environment too.

Leonardo's stone iconography is rooted in the Jewish religion and a number of biblical passages, in particular, in the *Book of Exodus* and St. John the Apostle's *Revelation*.

---

1 In *De divine proportione* Luca Pacioli gives the painting completion date at February 9, 1498; M. Bernardi, *Leonardo in Milano*, Torino 1952, p. 92; C. Baroni, S. Samek Ludovici, *La pittura lombarda del Quattrocento*, Messina-Firenze 1952, p. 337.
2 Mt 26,21 (ESVUK).
3 P. Lippini, *Furono i Domenicani a salvarlo dopo il bombardamento dell'agosto 1943*, in *L'Ultima Cena di Leonardo da Vinci. Una lettura storica, artistica e spirituale del grande capolavoro*, Comunità dei Padri Domenicani di Santa Maria delle Grazie, Milano s.d.; in-depth analysis, L. H. Heydenreich, *Invito a Leonardo: l'Ultima Cena*, Milano 1982.

Precious stones in the biblical and Christian tradition

The precious stones in Leonardo's *Last Supper* were well known to all the peoples of antiquity from the Egyptians to the Greeks. But we must bear in mind that ancient gemology did not classify minerals in the same way as today. The classification in use today takes into account colour, hardness, transparency and degree of refraction and clearly distinguishes precious (diamond, sapphire, ruby, and emerald), semi-precious (quartz, aquamarine, topaz, etc.) and hard (aggregates of various kinds) stones and organic substances (amber, coral, pearl).

In ancient civilizations, and long before Christ, every stone was considered valuable. Minerals were used in many areas of human life and had specific religious and magical meanings. On the basis of the presence or absence of certain requirements (colour, shape, light and transparency) stones were used in peoples' everyday lives and for the care of body and soul as each mineral was associated with certain virtues and specific properties. In addition to their therapeutic powers, from the fourth millennium BC Sumerians, Assyrians and Babylonians also linked the powers of such stones to cosmic astrological cycles to the extent that the Chaldeans named the planets after the minerals associated with them.

Certainly, even in ancient times, not everyone was convinced of the healing powers of minerals. For example, Pliny the Elder (23-79 A.D.) in his *Naturalis Historia* and citing numerous examples, considered them a deception by charlatans. He did not, however, fail to define gems 'majesty of nature, according to many people, the most beautiful in any part, so that the eyes of many for a total and complete contemplation of nature is sufficient by itself to any single gem'[4]. In general, however, stones were considered bearers of divine and spiritual values[5] and it was believed that they formed in places inaccessible to man. Invisible by day but shining in the darkness, for the men of antiquity gems were surrounded with an aura of mystery and a stone's value was proportional to the degree of secrecy it was suffused with. The profound separation between man and precious stones was underlined by the fact of the latter being transported from heaven to earth by birds[6].

Coming mainly from Middle Eastern countries, stones were cut following to two essential procedures, namely:

- cabochon, achieving a convex and oval-shaped stone;
- or facet, a suitable cut of the crystalline stones.

The carving of the gem by metal spikes on the back of the object, reporting on its surface or profane sacred symbols that enhanced their influences, it

---

4 C. Plinio, *Naturalis Historia*, translation by K. F. T. Mayhoff, Lipsiae, Teubner 1906, XXXVII, 1.
5 As remembered by Father Matteo La Grua in *Cristo nelle pietre preziose, per una rilettura biblica*, Palermo 1998, p. 12, in the Bible; 'Israel stone' (II Sam 23,3; Dt 32,4; Is 30,29); 'Eternal stone' (Is 26,4).
6 S. Macrì, *Pietre viventi. I minerali nell'immaginario del mondo antico*, Torino 2009, p. 83 f.

increased the value. Cut and engraved, the stone was set for the frame, which was performed by a skilled craftsman[7]. In the kingdoms of Israel, minerals were not available and people resorted to import them from neighbouring countries. Probably, the stones were only polished, as a step of *Exodus* says 'If you make me an altar of stone, you shall not build it of hewn stones, for if you wield your tool on it you profane it'[8].

The stones are mentioned for the first time in *Genesis* in reference to the twelve sons of Jacob, progenitors of the tribes, where it is said that Jacob gathered his sons to remain united and not mingled with the Egyptians. The names appear from the first-born, the youngest son: Reuben, Simeon, Levi, Judah, Zebulun, Issachar, Dan, Gad, Naphtali, Asher, Joseph, Benjamin:

Then Jacob called his sons and said, «Gather yourselves together, that I may tell you what shall happen to you in days to come. Assemble and listen, O sons of Jacob, listen to Israel your father. Reuben, you are my firstborn, my might, and the firstfruits of my strength, pre-eminent in dignity and pre-eminent in power. Unstable as water, you shall not have pre-eminence, because you went up to your father's bed; then you defiled it – he went up to my couch! Simeon and Levi are brothers; weapons of violence are their swords. Let my soul come not into their council; O my glory, be not joined to their company. For in their anger they killed men, and in their wilfulness they hamstrung oxen. Cursed be their anger, for it is fierce, and their wrath, for it is cruel! I will divide them in Jacob and scatter them in Israel. Judah, your brothers shall praise you; your hand shall be on the neck of your enemies; your father's sons shall bow down before you. Judah is a lion's cub; from the prey, my son, you have gone up. He stooped down; he crouched as a lion and as a lioness; who dares rouse him. The sceptre shall not depart from Judah, nor the ruler's staff from between his feet, until tribute comes to him; and to him shall be the obedience of the peoples. Binding his foal to the vine and his donkey's colt to the choice vine, he has washed his garments in wine and his vesture in the blood of grapes. His eyes are darker than wine, and his teeth whiter than milk. Zebulun shall dwell at the haven of the sea; and he shall be for an haven of ships; and his border shall be unto Zidon. Issachar is a strong ass couching down between two burdens: And he saw that rest was good, and the land that it was pleasant; and bowed his shoulder to bear, and became a servant unto tribute. Dan shall judge his people, as one of the tribes of Israel. Dan shall be a serpent by the way, an adder in the path, that biteth the horse heels, so that his rider shall fall backward. I have waited for thy salvation, O Lord. Gad, a troop shall overcome him: but he shall overcome at the last. Out of Asher his bread shall be fat, and he shall yield royal dainties. Naphtali is a hind let loose: he giveth goodly words. Joseph is a fruitful bough, even a fruitful bough by a well; whose branches run over the wall: The archers have sorely grieved him, and shot at him, and hated him: but his bow abode in strength, and the arms of his hands

---

7 C. Piglione, F. Tasso, item 'Glittologia', in *Arti minori*, Milano 2000, p. 153.
8 Ex 20,25 (ESVUK).

were made strong by the hands of the mighty God of Jacob; from thence is the shepherd, the stone of Israel: even by the God of thy father, who shall help thee; and by the Almighty, who shall bless thee with blessings of heaven above, blessings of the deep that lieth under, blessings of the breasts, and of the womb: the blessings of thy father have prevailed above the blessings of my progenitors unto the utmost bound of the everlasting hills: they shall be on the head of Joseph, and on the crown of the head of him that was separate from his brethren. Benjamin shall ravin as a wolf: in the morning he shall devour the prey, and at night he shall divide the spoil». All these are the twelve tribes of Israel: and this is it that their father spake unto them, and blessed them; every one according to his blessing he blessed them[9].

The names of the sons of Jacob are back in *Exodus* 28, which describes the *ephod*, the robe of the high priest from Aronne, packaged on the particulars that Yahweh gave Moses.

Then bring near to you Aaron your brother, and his sons with him, from among the people of Israel, to serve me as priests — Aaron and Aaron's sons, Nadab and Abihu, Eleazar and Ithamar. And you shall make holy garments for Aaron your brother, for glory and for beauty you shall speak to all the skilful, whom I have filled with a spirit of skill, that they make Aaron's garments to consecrate him for my priesthood. These are the garments they are to make: a chestpiece, an ephod, a robe, a patterned tunic, a turban, and a sash. They are to make these sacred garments for your brother, Aaron, and his sons to wear when they serve me as priests. So give them fine linen cloth, gold thread, and blue, purple, and scarlet thread.

Design of the Ephod.
The craftsmen must make the ephod of finely woven linen and skillfully embroider it with gold and with blue, purple, and scarlet thread.It will consist of two pieces, front and back, joined at the shoulders with two shoulder-pieces.The decorative sash will be made of the same materials: finely woven linen embroidered with gold and with blue, purple, and scarlet thread. Take two onyx stones, and engrave on them the names of the tribes of Israel. Six names will be on each stone, arranged in the order of the births of the original sons of Israel. Engrave these names on the two stones in the same way a jeweler engraves a seal. Then mount the stones in settings of gold filigree. Fasten the two stones on the shoulderpieces of the ephod as a reminder that Aaron represents the people of Israel. Aaron will carry these names on his shoulders as a constant reminder whenever he goes before the Lord. Make the settings of gold filigree,then braid two cords of pure gold and attach them to the filigree settings on the shoulders of the ephod[10].

9   Gn 49,1-28 (ESVUK). For the blessings of Jacob see Rufino di Concordia, *Le benedizioni dei patriarchi*, trans. edited by M. Veronese, Roma 1995.

10 Ex 28,1-14 (ESVUK).

The clothing of the high priest consisted basically of a tunic with trousers, a coat with belt, from the *ephod*, the breastplate ('*breastpiece*' in the Bible) with the humeral joints, also of cloth and the headdress with tiara. The *ephod* was initially a simple bodice closed at the front but later it took on greater symbolic value to the point of being packed with purple fabric and with thin gold stripes insertion. In *Exodus* we read that God gave Moses precise information not only on the packaging of the priestly robe, but also on the 'breastplate of justice, also called 'rational'[11], in Hebrew *hòshen* (perhaps resulting from *hòçen*,'breast')[12]. Worn over the *ephod*, the rational consisted of a square board of twenty centimeters side, adorned with four rows of three precious stones each, so twelve in total (figg. 5 and 6). The stones were engraved with the names of the tribes, and were placed in bezels applied to the rational, worn on the vest at chest level. In this way, the twelve names attached on the breastplate indicate the preciousness of Israel in God's eyes, who carried his people both on his shoulders and on his heart: symbol of light and integrity, the *urim* and the *thummim*, consisted perhaps of two precious stones on the shoulders of the high priest[13]. The Bible reminds them in order to consult the divine oracle[14], and according to the *Leviticus*[15] they were part of the High Priest's robe. In obedience to the divine order, Moses made stones that were embed in the breastplate of his brother, so the ornament was also called 'breastplate of the high priest Aaron'. The twelve stones correspond therefore to the twelve sons of Jacob and their respective tribes of Israel, and they come in succession on the rational from right to left, distributed in four horizontal rows called 'registers':

You shall make a breastpiece of judgement, in skilled work. In the style of the ephod you shall make it – of gold, blue and purple and scarlet yarns, and fine twined linen shall you make it. Foursquare it shall be being doubled; a span shall be the length thereof, and a span shall be the breadth thereof. And thou shalt set in it settings of stones, even four rows of stones: the first row shall be a sardius, a topaz, and a carbuncle: this shall be the first row. And the second row shall be an emerald, a sapphire, and a diamond. And the third row a ligure, an agate, and an amethyst. And the fourth row a beryl, and an onyx, and a jasper: they shall be set in gold in their inclosings. And the stones shall be with the names of the children of Israel, twelve, according to their names, like the engravings of a signet; every one with his name shall they be according to the twelve tribes[16].

11   J. T. Lienhard, *Ministry*, Eugene, Oregon 2011, p 64 f.
12   E. Zolli, *Israele, studi storico-religiosi*, Udine 1935, p. 186.
13   Ex 28,9-12.
14   Ex 28, 30.
15   Lv 8,8.
16   Ex 28,15-21 The arrangement of gemstones follows the order written of the Hebrew language. Such a distribution is given in Ex 39,8-14.

As for the association of the twelve tribes on the breastplate stones, the rabbinical tradition considers the order of birth of Jacob's sons, rather than the order in which their names appear in Gen 49[17]. Jacob had children, indeed, by four different women: Lia gave birth to Ruben, Simeon, Levi, Judah; then Dan and Naphtali were born, Bilhah's sons, Rachel's servant (Leah's younger sister); Zilpah, Leah's servant, gave birth to Gad and Asher; then the two younger sons of Leah, Issachar and Zebulun were born. Finally, Jacob, who was elder by now, had Joseph and Benjamin by his wife Rachel (see diagram below). With this sequence, the corresponding stones appear to adorn the hòshen according to rabbinic tradition, which tends to change only the order of the arrangement, rather than the association between the stones and the tribes that tends to remain constant.

12 Sons / Tribes	Names' meaning	Mother
1. Reuben	Because the Lord has seen my affliction	Leah
2. Simeon	Because the Lord has heard that I am unloved	Leah
3. Levi	Be joined	Leah
4. Judah	Praise	Leah
5. Dan	God has judged me	Bilhah
6. Naphtali	To twist	Bilhah
7. Gad	To cut	Zilpah
8. Asher	To go straight on	Zilpah
9. Issachar	A man	Leah
10. Zebulon	To exalt or honor	Leah
11. Joseph	To add or increase	Rachel
12. Benjamin	Son	Rachel

Even St. Epiphanius, bishop of Salamis who lived in the fourth century, in the Treaty De XII gemmis he wrote at the request of the bishop of Tyre Diodorus[18], reported a version of the chest that, according to the rabbinical criteria, associates each stone to one of Jacob's sons in order of birth. According to Ladner, Epiphanius relied on antique books about stones, also to the descriptions of Clement of Alexandria, and he did not just talked about the healing properties of

---

17 Gen 49,1-28.
18 Rosa Conte wrote that other authors as Girolamo da Stridone, Procopio da Gaza, Facondo vescovo di Ermiana e Anastasio Sinaita knew this text, *Epiphanius von Salamis, Uber die zwolf Steine im hohepries-terlichen Brustschild (De duodecim gemmis rationalis): nach dem "Codex Vaticanus Borgianus Armenus"* (2014), in AA.VV., *Erga-Logoi*, Vol. 3, No. 2 (2015): *Rivista di Storia, Letteratura, Diritto e culture dell'antichità*, p. 203.

minerals and meaning but he focused on the association between the twelve stones of the rational and the tribes of Israel, attributing to each gem a particular supernatural significance[19].

Usually one considers the cap. 49 of Genesis, which lists the founders as regards as the mother (for Leah and Rachel), while the sons of the handmaids appear in order of birth. According to this criterion, the sequence of names is as follows: Reuben, Simeon, Levi, Judah, Issachar and Zebulun (Leah's sons); Dan and Gad (the first son of Bila, the second of Zilpah); Naftali, and Asher (idem); Joseph and Benjamin (Rachel's sons). Therefore, according to the adopted criterion of citation and in relation to the different classification of gemstones, which were distinguished in antiquity more for the colour than for their mineral species, many versions of the breastplate have spread. Moreover, the different Bible translations have to be added, as they also describe other stones. For example, instead of ruby, placed at the beginning of the second register, the Jerusalem Bible quotes turquoise. We must also bear in mind that Egyptian amulets were much appreciated and exported all over the Mediterranean basin[20], to the extent that in designs for hòshen, the Jewish breastplate worn by high priests, the Jews were perhaps inspired by the golden breastplates worn by the pharaohs[21], also embellished with precious stones of all kinds in addition to the Egyptian shen, an ancient amulet also used in Mesopotamia as a symbol of divinity[22].

The Jews' knowledge about constellations was perhaps brief[23]; however, considering that astrology was born in Chaldea[24] (the Jews were exiled there in VII-VI cent. BC), and that the Zodiac began to spread in the sixth century BC, the Jews probably came to know it and it is conceivable that the same rationale was adorned with a number of stones corresponding, besides Jacob's children, also to the Zodiac signs, as the gems that adorned the high priest's vest which referred to the seven planetary spheres[25]. According to Hani, the Jewish cosmic symbolism married to the mystical, because the Jewish tradition related the tribes of Israel to the zodiac signs[26]. In this venue, we are considering the version of the hòshen with the gem-

19 G. B. Ladner, *Il simbolismo paleocristiano. Dio, cosmo, uomo*, Milano 2008, p. 153.

20 J. M. Rivière, *Amuleti, Talismani e Pantacoli, I principi e la scienza dei Talismani, nelle tradizioni orientali e occidentali*, trans. edited by D. Rossi, Roma 1994, p. 59.

21 G. Cereseto, *Istituzioni bibliche, ossia introduzione generale e speciale a tutti i libri della Santa Scrittura*, Chiavari 1893, p. 165.

22 E. Zolli, *Israele*, cit., pp. 49 e 185.

23 In-depth analysis on astronomy in ancient times, G. V. Schiapparelli, *Scritti sulla storia della astronomia antica*, vol. 2, Milano 1998.

24 Most of the Greek names of the constellations of the Zodiac derived from the corresponding Babylonian names, G. V. Schiaparelli, *Scritti sulla storia della astronomia antica*, vol. 2, Milano 1998, p. 354.

25 S. Cavenago-Bignami, *Gemmologia*, Tomo I, Milano 1980, p. 144.

26 J. Hani, *Il simbolismo del tempio cristiano*, trans. edited by T. Buonacerva, Paris 1978, p. 71.

tribe relationship that I was shown by the 'Jewish' section of the Jewish Museum in London[27], in the order in which the names of the twelve sons of Jacob appear in Genesis 49,3-27: Reuben, Simeon, Levi, Judah, Issachar, Zebulun, Dan, Gad, Naphtali, Asher, Joseph and Benjamin. With this sequence the corresponding stones appear on rational according to the most common version of the breastplate [28].

27   I thank Mrs Sarah Harel Hoshen (Jewish Museum, London). Taking account of its biblical version, the ruby is mentioned, instead of turquoise.
28   In-depth analysis, F. Piro, *La tenda del deserto, Architettura* del *primo santuario di Israele*, Lecce 2014.

I REGISTER

The gems of the breastplate.

The first stone cited in Exodus 28 is odhem[29], the carnelian, also called 'Sardinian' or 'sardonic' (see figg. 5 and 6), a chalcedony belonging to the family of quartz, semi-transparent, with red-orange reflections or rust due to the presence of iron oxides. Imported from Arabia and Persia, it was much appreciated by the ancient people.

Theophrastus distinguishes the Sardinian 'female', which was clearer, from the Sardinian 'male', darker[30]. The Egyptians believed it was actually the symbol of Isis's blood[31], and so it was sacred to the goddess who recomposed the body of Osiris to allow him to raise again; therefore, for its red colour, carnelian has always been associated with the sun and the blood[32], and considered capable of eliminating any fear, even that of death: for example, in Etruscan area it was probably cut in scarab's shape and worn at the neck by warriors[33]. During the early Christian age, it became a symbol of sacrifice, and was believed to be reddened with the blood of martyrs[34]. For the red colour, it was confused with ruby; however, the stone that appeared on the rational could not be a ruby, very rare and too tiny to engrave. Related from the Babylonian astrology to the sign of Gemini and the planet of Mercury[35], in the hòshen the carnelian opens the I register, at the top right. It symbolizes the tribe of Reu'vén (Reuben) and it corresponds in Kabbalah to the noun Melek, which means 'king'[36]. It refers to Justice, and is mentioned in Ex 28,17; Ex 39,10; Rev 4,3; Rev 21,20.

---

29 M. G. La Grua, *Cristo nelle pietre preziose*, Roma 1998, p. 32.
30 Presentation edited by A. Mottana, *Il libro sulle pietre di Teofrasto*, translation edited by M. Napolitano, Roma 1997, p. 162.
31 I. Maserri Bencini, *L'Egitto secondo gli scrittori antichi e moderni*, Firenze 1912, p. 153.
32 S. Cavenago-Bignami, *Gemmologia*, cit., p. 864.
33 F. Inghirami, *Storia della Toscana compilata ed in sette epoche*, Fiesole 1841, p. 617.
34 S. Cavenago-Bignami, cit., p. 864.
35 H. Lammer, M. Y. Boudjada, *Enigmi di pietra. I misteri degli edifici medievali*, trad. di A. Manco, Roma 2005, pp. 62-63.
36 S. Cavenago-Bignami, *Gemmologia*, cit., p. 860.

5. Distribuzione delle dodici pietre sul pettorale del sommo sacerdote.
L'ordine segue la descrizione di *Esodo* 28,15-21 (Nuova Riveduta).
che riferisce il rubino alla tribù di Giuda.
*Distribution of the twelve stones on the Priestly breastplate, as you
read in Exodus 28,15-21, that relates the ruby to the tribe of Judah.*

6. Schema della distribuzione delle pietre sul pettorale in relazione alle dodici tribù e in relazione alla madre.
Scheme of distribution of the stones in relation to the twelve tribes and to the mothers.

The second stone in Exodus, pit'dah (or piteda)[37], indicates the topaz, a golden or reddish yellow aluminium fluorosilicate. It came from the island of Zeberged in the Red Sea [38], from Ethiopia, Arabia, Pakistan, India and Sri Lanka. The so-called 'Eastern Topaz' was instead a less valuable corundum[39]. We do not know, though, if the stone on the breastplate was the citrine, or the real topaz, in the yellowish variety. It may well be it was then known as chrysoprase or chrysolite, 'gold-coloured translucent' since Pliny mentions a green leek colour type[40], with rare hues in the topaz that, moreover, does not lend itself to be engraved. The mineral exists in nature even in the blue or greenish hue; less valuable, it came from the Urals where, for its colour, it was called 'Topaz-aquamarine'[41]. The Latin name topazius may derive from the Sanskrit tapas, 'heat'[42], because if heated, the stone changes color. In some ancient civilization it symbolized the sun[43], while the Babylonians relate it to the sign of Leo[44]. Considered miraculous, the topaz was worn as an amulet[45]. The Bible mentions it in Ex 28,17; Ex 39,10; Job 28,19; Ezek 1,16; Ezek 10,9; Ezek 28,12-13; Dn 10,6 and Rev 21,20. The prophet Daniel, speaking of the vision in which he contemplates the appearance of the Highest, says 'His body resembled topaz'[46]; even the wheels of the 'chariot of the Lord' in Ezekiel's vision are made of topaz[47]. The stone is placed on the left of the First register of carnelian, representing the tribe of Shim'eon (Simeon) and is associated in Kabbalah attribute divine Gomel, 'benefactor'[48].

The third gem is the emerald, from the Greek smàragdos, 'greenstone', beryllium and aluminium silicate. The Jews called it bareket, from barak, 'to shine'[49]. Gaio Sollio Sidonius Apollinaris called it 'scintille oculorum, cordis e incentiva'[50]. Prized mineral, symbol of harmony and hope, Pliny says that there were as many as twelve different quality, present in Upper Egypt, in Scythia and in

37   M. G. La Grua, *Cristo nelle pietre preziose,* Roma 1998, p. 32.
38   Pliny cites 'Topazo', an isle of the Red Sea (*Naturalis Historia,* cit., XXXVII, 37).
39   S. Cavenago-Bignami, *Gemmologia,* cit., p. 642.
40   C. Plinio, *Naturalis Historia,* cit., XXXVII, 37.
41   S. Cavenago-Bignami, *Gemmologia,* cit., p. 650.
42   M. Biniecka, *Gemme e oro: aspetti tecnologici, qualitativi, economici e sociali,* Consiglio Nazionale delle Ricerche, Roma 2004, p. 170.
43   M. Mantovani, *Meditazioni sull'albero della Cabala,* Milano 2002, p. 175.
44   H. Lammer, M. Y. Boudjada, Enigmi di pietra, cit., pp. 62-63
45   E. Villiers, *Amuleti, talismani ed altre cose misteriose,* Milano 1995, p. 352.
46   Dn 10,6.
47   Ezek 1,16.
48   S. Cavenago-Bignami, *Gemmologia,* cit., p. 860.
49   M. G. La Grua, *Cristo nelle pietre preziose,* cit., p. 33.
50   Sidonio Apollinare, *Epistolae,* I, 8, 12, 46.

Cyprus and that it was useful for the eyes[51]. Theophrastus too[52] believed it was useful for eye diseases and it had the power to transmit its own colour to the water[53]. In the ancient civilizations, it was associated with the planet Venus and the sign of Taurus[54]. It corresponded to the tribe of Levi, while in the Kabbalah postponed attribute divine Adar, 'Magnificent'[55]. In the Bible the emerald is mentioned in Ex 28,17; Ex 39,10; Tb 13,17; Jdt 10,21; Sir 32,6; Is 54,12; Ezek 28,13; Rev 4,3.

51 C. Plinio, *Naturalis Historia*, cit., XXXVII, 20-21; Cavenago-Bignami, *Gemmologia*, cit. pp. 658 e 662.
52 Theophrastus (372-287 BC is the author of *On Stones* (315 BC), the first treaty on mineralogy that is known.
53 A. Mottana, *Il libro sulle pietre di Teofrasto*, cit., p. 161; C. Plinio, *Naturalis Historia*, cit., XXXVII, 20.
54 H. Lammer, M. Y. Boudjada, *Enigmi di pietra*, cit., pp. 62-63.
55 S. Cavenago-Bignami, *Gemmologia*, cit., p. 860.

II REGISTER

The second register opens with ruby, the Hebrew nophek[56], prized Corundum since ancient times. Theophrastus believed it was incombustible[57], enough to be translated anthrax, 'burning coal', from the Latin Vulgate[58]. Related to the Sun by the Indian culture[59], the Jews associated the tribe of Yehudah (Judah) and the divine attribute Eloah, 'Great Lord'[60]. Later, as Ladner recalled, Epiphanius of Salamis joined the irradiation of red mineral to the blood of Christ and the fire of the Pentecostal Spirit[61]. However, we know that the ancient confused the stones of the same colour, as until the Middle Ages, it was the main parameter for distinguishing between a mineral and another. Therefore, despite the rarity of the stone, any reddish mineral was called nophek. The confusion was about carnelian, red jasper and carbuncle, an oxide of the quartz group, that Babylonian astrology associated to the sign of Capricorn and the planet Saturn[62], for its resemblance to the fire[63], as it was considered capable of stimulating values such as perseverance and wisdom in the corresponding astrological sign.

The Bible CEI mentions the ruby rather than the turquoise, aluminium phosphate and blue-green copper that was also related to the tribe of Judah[64]. As amethyst and aquamarine, turquoise was associated with the zodiac sign of Libra and the planet Venus[65], which was believed to bring optimism, harmony and balance. Turquoise is mentioned in Ex 28,18; Ex 39,11; Tb 13,17.

The fifth stone is the sapphire, Hebrew sappir[66], 'the best thing'. Pliny the Elder mentions the excellent quality of that coming from Media, despite being

---

56   M. G. La Grua, *Cristo nelle pietre preziose,* cit., p. 34. In other Bibles *nophek* is referred to turquoise (*La Bibbia: Antico Testamento*, Ed. Paoline, Roma 1991, p. 285); *La tenda del deserto, architettura del primo santuario di Israele,* Lecce 2014, p. 166.

57   Presentation by A. Mottana, *Il libro sulle pietre di Teofrasto,* Translation by M. Napolitano, Roma 1997, p. 182.

58   M. G. La Grua, *Cristo nelle pietre preziose*, cit., p. 34.

59   S. Cavenago-Bignami, *Gemmologia,* cit., p. 496.

60   S. Cavenago-Bignami, *Gemmologia,* cit., p. 860.

61   G. B. Ladner, Il simbolismo paleocristiano, cit., p. 153.

62   H. Lammer, M. Y. Boudjada, *Enigmi di pietra,* cit., pp. 62-63.

63   C. Plinio, *Naturalis Historia,* cit., XXXVII, 32; S. Cavenago-Bignami, *Gemmologia,* cit., p. 496.

64   S..Cavenago-Bignami,..*Gemmologia,*.cit.,..p..860...For..further..details,..see: A. Lipinsky, *Oro, argento, gemme e smalti: tecnologia delle arti dalle origini alla fine del Medioevo, 3000 a.C. - 1500 d.C*, Florence 1975, p. 395 s.

65   H. Lammer, M. Y. Boudjada, *Enigmi di pietra,* cit., pp. 62-63.

66   treccani.it/vocabolario/zaffiro/ (last visit: 22.08.2016).

unfit to engrave[67]. The aluminum trioxide was used to treat ophthalmia to the eyes[68] and bites of scorpions. The Jews considered it a sacred stone, in relation to a step in the Exodus:

Then Moses and Aaron, Nadab, and Abihu, and seventy of the elders of Israel went up and they saw the God of Israel. There was under his feet as it were a pavement of sapphire stone, like the very heaven for clearness[69].

However, when John wrote the Book of Revelation in the first century AD, the word referred to as lapis lazuli, and also Pliny citing sappirus actually referred to lapis lazuli[70]. Probably this was the stone mentioned in Exodus[71], a mineral with a strong cosmological value, whose blue was associated with the world of deep introspection, to starry sky, and then it was associated to the Blessed Virgin[72]. On the breastplate the stone refers to the tribe of Yisascar (Issachar). In the Kabbalah corresponds to the divine attribute Hain, which means 'source', 'eye'[73], and it is associated with the planet Jupiter and the sign of Sagittarius[74]. Sapphire is mentioned in Ex 24,10; Ex 28,18; Ex 39,11; Tb 13,17; Job 28,16; Ezek 1,26; Ezek 10,1; Rev 21,19:

Then I looked, and behold, on the expanse that was over the heads of the cherubim there appeared above them something like a sapphire, in appearance like a throne[75].

The sixth stone, from Hebrew Yahalom or jahalon, translated as 'diamond'[76], is a compound of carbon atoms crystallized into a tetrahedral structure. It was mainly imported from India, Arabia and Cyprus. Pliny wrote that in human affairs, and not only among gems, it was considered of the greatest value and was

---

67   C. Plinio, *Naturalis Historia,* cit., XXXVII, 40.

68   S. Macrì, *Pietre viventi,* cit., p. 93; Cavenago-Bignami, cit., p. 496.

69   Ex 24,9-10.

70   F. Piro, *La tenda nel deserto,* cit., p. 168; C. Plinio, *Naturalis Historia,* cit., XVII, 40. Pliny recalls that the Sapphire did not lend itself to receive incisions.

71   M. G. La Grua, *Cristo nelle pietre preziose,* cit., p. 35.

72   In the Bible the blue of the two stones was considered sacred and regal, in F. Berdini, *La Gioconda chi è,* Roma 1989, p. 78; M. G. La Grua, *Cristo nelle pietre preziose,* cit., p. 35.; F. Cervini, C. Spantigati, *Il tempo di Pio V, Pio V nel tempo: atti del Convegno internazionale di studi,* Bosco Marengo, Alessandria 2006, p. 348. For the Last Supper's astrology, the text of F. Berdini is suggested, *Magia e astrologia in Leonardo,* Roma, 1982.

73   S. Cavenago-Bignami, *Gemmologia,* cit., p. 860. For further details, see: A. Lipinsky, *Oro, argento, gemme e smalti: tecnologia delle arti dalle origini alla fine del Medioevo, 3000 a.C. - 1500 d.C,* Florence 1975, p. 395 f.

74   H. Lammer, M. Y. Boudjada, *Enigmi di pietra,* cit., p. 63

75   Ezek 10,1.

76   For an in-depth analysis see F. Di Giovambattista, *Il Giorno dell'espiazione nella Lettera agli Ebrei,* Roma 2000, pp. 63-65.

long known only to kings. He categoriṣed diamonds according to their different origins such as Ethiopia, India, Arabia and Cyprus and noted the ability of such stones to neutralise poisons and drive delusions and vain fears from the mind[77]. In the Kabbalah, this corresponds to the Elchai 'living God'[78] attribute. The Bible mentions it in Jer 17,1; Ezek 3,9; Zech 7,12. The diamond is a reference to the tribe of Zevulun (Zebulun) and as Stefania Macioce has noted, the high priest wore it three times a year (at Easter, Pentecost and the Feast of Tabernacles) when he entered the Sancta Sanctorum[79]. The stone was linked in this context to the Cancer star sign and the Moon[80], a reference to adularia, the moonstone[81], with emotion and deep feelings associations.

The stone on the breastplate however was not a diamond, which could not be engraved, but quartz or beryl, a sometimes colourless aluminum silicate. Beryl, confused with aquamarine[82], was used in rituals to propitiate the rain and the water-related ones[83]. It was also worn during navigation to protect oneself from drowning and storms. The Bible mentions it in Ex 28,28; Ex 39,11; Job 28,16; Rev 21,20. Beryl refers to the planet Mercury and the sign of Virgo[84].

77   C. Plinio, *Naturalis Historia,* cit., XXXVII, 18.
78   S. Cavenago-Bignami, *Gemmologia,* cit., p. 860.
79   S. Macioce, *Ori nell'arte: per una storia del potere segreto delle gemme,* Roma 2007, p. 137; A. Bacci, *Delle XII pietre pretiose, le quali per ordine di Dio nella santa legge adornavano la veste sacra del Sommo Sacerdote,* Roma 1587, p. 18.
80   H. Lammer, M. Y. Boudjada, *Enigmi di pietra,* cit., p. 63.
81   The moonstone, white with light blue reflexs, was a very appreciated stone (treccani.it/vocabolario/adularia/ - last visit: 31.08.2016).
82   Pliny distinguishes two types of beryllium, one of the most intense color, and a lighter properly so called 'Beryl', Naturalis Historia, cit., XXXVII, 25.
83   S. Macrì, *Pietre viventi,* cit., p. 95.
84   H. Lammer, M. Y. Boudjada, *Enigmi di pietra,* cit., p. 63.

III REGISTER

The seventh stone, *lesham* or *lesem*, is translated *ligurius* from the Latin[85]. The modern gemology does not identify the *ligurius*; it is perhaps amber as mentioned by Pliny[86], or hyacinth, fine orange zircon tending to violet. The best pieces came from Ethiopia[87]. However, there is also the variety of blue zircon, one of the colours used in the vest of the high priest and the temple in Jerusalem[88]. In the *hòshen*, hyacinth opens the III register, it represents the tribe of Dan and, according to the Kabbalah, it corresponds to the divine attribute *Elohim*, 'God'[89].

The mineral is mentioned in the Bible in Ex 28,19; Ex 39,12; Sir 45,10; Rev 9,17; Rev 21,20. The hyacinth refers to the planets of Pluto and Mars, governors of the sign of Scorpio[90], which was believed to donate the sense of mystery and determination.

The eighth stone, *shebuw* (or *sebo*)[91], was perhaps the agate, banded variety of chalcedony with circles of different colours. Used for incisions, in gemmology the chalcedony indicates a large amount of crystals of a different colour. In the rational, the stone follows the hyacinth in the third register, and refers to the tribe of Gad; according to Kabbalah, it refers to the divine attribute *El*, 'strong'[92]. In the Bible the agate is mentioned in Ex 28,19; Ex 39,12. Pliny distinguished different types from different areas; from Sicily, where according to the writer, it was found the first time, from Crete, Egypt, Phrygia, Cyprus, Rhodes and India. Pliny also wrote that it was believed that once the stone was placed in the mouth it alleviated thirst, it was useful for sight, it was effective against the bites of spiders and scorpions, and it warded off lightning, storms and waterspouts[93]. The agate is associated with the sign of Virgo related to Mercury[94], the planet linked to the values of intelligence, analysis and organization. Interestingly, four of the twelve

---

85 M. G. La Grua, *Cristo nelle pietre preziose*, cit., p. 38. Pliny also mentions the lyncurio, stone that has the color of amber 'on fire' and that was carved (*Naturalis Historia*, cit., XXXVII, 16).

86 C. Plinio, *Naturalis Historia*, cit., XXXVII, 13. Pliny the Elder mentions that the farmers in the Celtic area traspadana wore amber necklaces whose purpose was ornamental and also medical.

87 C. Plinio, *Naturalis Historia*, cit., XXXVII, 42.

88 Ex 28,31.

89 S. Cavenago-Bignami, *Gemmologia*, cit., p. 860.

90 H. Lammer, M. Y. Boudjada, *Enigmi di pietra*, cit., p. 63.

91 M. G. La Grua, *Cristo nelle pietre preziose*, cit., p. 39.

92 S. Cavenago-Bignami, *Gemmologia*, cit., p. 860.

93 C. Plinio, *Naturalis Historia*, cit., XXXVII, 49.

94 H. Lammer, M. Y. Boudjada, *Enigmi di pietra*, cit., p. 63.

precious stones that adorn the rational belong to the family of chalcedony[95]: carnelian, agate, onyx, jasper.

The III register closes with *ahlamah* or *achlama*, identified with amethyst[96], a quartz that owes its violet colour to the presence of traces of iron. The minerals of a better quality came from Indus Valley, Egypt, Mesopotamia[97]. The stone put off the purple colour of the wine and its name derived from the greek *amethystos*, 'not drunk', because it was believed it would protect the state of drunkenness. Pliny also mentions the belief that amethyst kept away the evil, the storms and locusts[98]. In the *hòshen* amethyst refers to the tribe of *Naphtali* and according to the Kabbalah corresponds to the divine attribute *Iaho*, that is 'God'[99]. The Bible mentions it in Ex 28,19; Ex 39,12; Rev 21,20 (the stone adorns the twelfth foundation of the City). Amethyst is associated to the planet of Uranus that encourages inventiveness and idealism to the corresponding Zodiac sign of Aquarius[100].

---

95 White-blue colored mineral, if pure, it is composed of a quartz formed by aggregates of microscopic fibers. Several varieties can bedistinguished, some of which are used as semi-precious stones (treccani.it/enciclopedia/ calcedonio/ - last visit: 19.09.2016).
96 G. Busi, *Simboli del pensiero ebraico: lessico ragionato in settanta voci*, Torino 1999, p. 102; M. G. La Grua, *Cristo nelle pietre*, cit., p. 40.
97 C. Plinio, *Naturalis Historia*, cit., XXXVII, 41.
98 C. Plinio, *Naturalis Historia*, cit., XXXVII, 41.
99 S. Cavenago-Bignami, *Gemmologia*, cit., p. 860.
100 H. Lammer, M. Y. Boudjada, *Enigmi di pietra*, cit., p. 63.

IV REGISTER

The last register opens to the right with the tenth stone, tarshish, translated 'chrysolite'[101] from the greek 'golden stone', because of the colour tending to golden green. Also known as 'peridot', this iron and magnesium silicate was widespread in the Middle-East area, although according to Pliny the Elder, the better quality beryl came from Ethiopia, while the Arabs one were less valuable[102]. Pliny called it a translucent stone, with a golden colour, and he reported in turn the opinion of Callistratus as to the property to heal fever, and ear and eye disorders[103].

In the *hòshen* the chrysolite refers to the tribe of *Asher* (or Aser) and it corresponds to the divine attribute Ischgob, which means 'High God'[104]. The Bible mentions the stone in Ex 28,20; Ex 39,13; Rev 21,20. It was associated with the planet Neptune, that was believed to confer a sense of humanity and mysticism to its zodiac sign of Pisces.

The eleventh stone in Hebrew soham, 'to whiten', was translated 'onyx' from the Vulgate[105]. Chalcedony quartz was easy to be engraved, and it was widespread and used by the ancients for cameos and seals; it was located in Egypt, in the Arabian Peninsula and India[106]. A mineral of many and different colours, sometimes the onyx is confused with sardonyx, another type of quartz of reddish-brown colour. Very useful to find the right words in speeches and to induce love, it was thought to have the power to end disputes. It was associated with the planet of Saturn and the zodiac sign of Capricorn. In the hòshen, onyx is positioned in the fourth register and it refers to the tribe of Yosef (Joseph) and corresponds, according to the Kabbalah, to the divine attribute Adonai, 'Lord'[107]. It is mentioned in Gen 2,12; Ex 25,7; Ex 28,9.20; Ex 30,34; Ex 35,9.27; Ex 39,6.13; Sir 24,15.

The breastplate ends with the twelfth stone, yashfeh or jaspeh, translated 'jasper' by rabbinic tradition[108]. It is a chalcedony with iron oxides, which give it the blood-red colour; other times it presents itself of a greenish, red and green together, yellowish or brown coloration due to the presence of other types of

101 M. G. La Grua, *Cristo nelle pietre preziose,* cit., p. 40.
102 C. Plinio, *Naturalis Historia,* cit., XXXVII, 42.
103 C. Plinio, *Naturalis Historia,* cit., XXXVII, 15.
104 S. Cavenago-Bignami, *Gemmologia,* cit., p. 860.
105 M. G. La Grua, *Cristo nelle pietre preziose,* cit., p. 41.
106 C. Plinio, *Naturalis Historia,* cit., XXXVII, 30.
107 S. Cavenago-Bignami, *Gemmologia*, cit., p. 860.
108 According to P. M. La Grua, the translation of the Vulgata, *jaspeh,* could identify the beryl. In this case, the stone associated with the tribe of Zebulon was a jasper.

crystals. Pliny the Elder also writes of Indian green varieties similar to emerald[109]. Jasper was also located in India, Cyprus, Persia, Phrygia, Cappadocia, Egypt[110]. It was believed to stimulate energy and to favour a combative character. The Egyptians compared it to the blood of Isis[111], while the Jews associated it with the appelation YHWH, Yahweh, 'the Existing par excellence', 'the One who Is'[112]. In the breastplate, it is associated to the tribe of Binyamin (Benjamin). The Bible mentions the stone in Ex 28,20; Ex 39,13; Rev 4,3; Rev 21,11.18-19:

> *And he who sat there had the appearance of jasper and carnelian, and round the throne was a rainbow that had the appearance of an emerald[113].*

The quality of red jasper was related to Mars, the planet of force, and to the zodiac sign of Aries.

The Book of Revelation (21,20) also mentions the chrysoprase, associated with the planet Venus and the sign of Libra.

As noted, in addition to the name of the twelve tribes of Israel, each stone was associated with a divine attribute. This is the sequence of attributes, according to the succession of the stones in the breastplate: Melek (King), Gomel (who rewarns), Adar (the magnificent), Eloah (Strong God), Hain (eye), Elchai (Living God), Elohim (Strong Gods), El (the Strong), Iaho (God), Ischgob (High God), Adonai (the Lord), Ihovah (I am who I am). According to the Kabbalah, the twelve names of God were engraved on the stones placed in the rational; in the monotheistic culture the attributes indicate the only name of Yahweh, the Tetragrammaton יהוה, the God who was forever faithful to his people. The faithfulness of Israel, reflected in the breastplate of Aaron, will instead be put to test on many occasions, as in the challenge of Carmel: Elijah calls Ahab and the prophets of Baal, to show them that there is no other god before Yahweh:

> *So Ahab sent to all the people of Israel and gathered the prophets together at Mount Carmel. And Elijah came near to all the people and said, «How long will you go limping between two different opinions? If the Lord is God, follow him; but if Baal, then follow him». And the people did not answer him a word. Then Elijah said to the people, «I, even I only, am left a prophet of the Lord, but Baal's prophets are 450 men. Let two bulls be given to us, and let them choose one bull for themselves and cut it in pieces and lay it on the wood,*

109 C. Plinio, *Naturalis Historia,* cit., XXXVII, 40.
110 C. Plinio, *Naturalis Historia,* cit., XXXVII, 40; S. Lucchesi, *Archeogemmologia: le pietre nella Bibbia,* Testo della Conferenza, Torino 4 marzo 2003.
111 S. Cavenago-Bignami, *Gemmologia,* cit., p. 863.
112 treccani.it/enciclopedia/jahve (Enciclopedia Italiana)/(last visit:18.08.2016).
113 Rev 4,3.

but put no fire to it. I will prepare the other bull and lay it on the wood, but put no fire to it. And you call upon the name of your god, and I will call upon the name of the Lord, and the God who answers by fire, he is God». And all the people answered, «It is well spoken». Then Elijah said to the prophets of Baal, «Choose for yourselves one bull and prepare it first, for you are many; then call on the name of your god, but put no fire to it». So they took the bull that was given them, prepared it, and called on the name of Baal from morning until noon, crying, «O Baal, answer us!». But there was no voice, and no answer. They limped about the altar that they had made. At noon Elijah mocked them, saying, «Cry aloud! Surely he is a god; either he is meditating, or he has wandered away, or he is on a journey, or perhaps he is asleep and must be awakened». Then they cried aloud and, as was their custom, they cut themselves with swords and lances until the blood gushed out over them. As midday passed, they raved on until the time of the offering of the oblation, but there was no voice, no answer, and no response. Then Elijah said to all the people, «Come closer to me»; and all the people came closer to him. First he repaired the altar of the Lord that had been thrown down; Elijah took twelve stones, according to the number of the tribes of the sons of Jacob, to whom the word of the Lord came, saying, «Israel shall be your name»; with the stones he built an altar in the name of the Lord. Then he made a trench around the altar, large enough to contain two measures of seed. Next he put the wood in order, cut the bull in pieces, and laid it on the wood. He said, «Fill four jars with water and pour it on the burnt offering and on the». Then he said, «Do it a second time»; and they did it a second time. Again he said, «Do it a third time»; and they did it a third time, so that the water ran all around the altar, and filled the trench also with water. At the time of the offering of the oblation, the prophet Elijah came near and said, «O Lord, God of Abraham, Isaac, and Israel, let it be known this day that you are God in Israel, that I am your servant, and that I have done all these things at your bidding. Answer me, O Lord, answer me, so that this people may know that you, O Lord, are God, and that you have turned their hearts back». Then the fire of the Lord fell and consumed the burnt offering, the wood, the stones, and the dust, and even licked up the water that was in the trench. When all the people saw it, they fell on their faces and said, «The Lord indeed is God; the Lord indeed is God»[114].

The text reaffirms the membership of Israel to God in relation to the breastplate, remembering that 'Elijah took twelve stones, one for each of the tribes descended from Jacob' and with them he built the new altar to God; the altar is the

---

114 1Kings 18,20-39.

heart of man, which agrees to be a place consecrated to Yahweh. This was also the reason why the breastplate was worn on the chest.

Nine of the twelve stones mentioned in Exodus 28 also appear in the Book of Ezekiel[115], albeit in a different order: rubies, topaz, diamond, beryl, onyx, jasper, sapphires, emeralds and carbuncles. The different translations, the Greek Septuagint and the Latin Vulgate, have suggested different identifications of minerals (see after IV Register). The Book of Revelation also speaks of the twelve stones, albeit in a different order:

Then came one of the seven angels who had the seven bowls full of the seven last plagues and spoke to me, saying, «Come, I will show you the Bride, the wife of the Lamb». And he carried me away in the Spirit to a great, high mountain, and showed me the holy city Jerusalem coming down out of heaven from God, having the glory of God, its radiance like a most rare jewel, like a jasper, clear as crystal. It had a great, high wall, with twelve gates, and at the gates twelve angels, and on the gates the names of the twelve tribes of the sons of Israel were inscribed – on the east three gates, on the north three gates, on the south three gates, and on the west three gates. And the wall of the city had twelve foundations, and on them were the twelve names of the twelve apostles of the Lamb. The angel who talked to me had a measuring rod of gold to measure the city and its gates and walls. The city lies foursquare, its length the same as its width; and he measured the city with his rod, fifteen hundred miles; its length and width and height are equal. He also measured its wall, one hundred forty-four cubits by human measurement, which the angel was using. The wall is built of jasper, while the city is pure gold, clear as glass. The foundations of the wall of the city are adorned with every jewel; the first was jasper, the second sapphire, the third agate, the fourth emerald, the fifth onyx, the sixth carnelian, the seventh chrysolite, the eighth beryl, the ninth topaz, the tenth chrysoprase, the eleventh jacinth, the twelfth amethyst. And the twelve gates are twelve pearls, each of the gates is a single pearl, and the street of the city is pure gold, transparent as glass. I saw no temple in the city, for its temple is the Lord God the Almighty and the Lamb. And the city has no need of sun or moon to shine on it, for the glory of God is its light, and its lamp is the Lamb. The nations will walk by its light, and the kings of the earth will bring their glory into it. Its gates will never be shut by day – and there will be no night there. People will bring into it the glory and the honor of the nations.

115 Ezek 28,11-22.

But nothing unclean will enter it, nor anyone who practices abomination or falsehood, but only those who are written in the Lamb's book of life[116].

The description of Revelation is inspired by the Book of Ezekiel:

These shall be the exits of the city: On the north side, which is to be 4,500 cubits by measure, three gates, the gate of Reuben, the gate of Judah, and the gate of Levi, the gates of the city being named after the tribes of Israel. On the east side, which is to be 4,500 cubits, three gates, the gate of Joseph, the gate of Benjamin, and the gate of Dan. On the south side, which is to be 4,500 cubits by measure, three gates, the gate of Simeon, the gate of Issachar, and the gate of Zebulun. On the west side, which is to be 4,500 cubits, three gates, the gate of Gad, the gate of Asher, and the gate of Naphtali. The circumference of the city shall be 18,000 cubits. And the name of the city from that time on shall be, 'The Lord Is There'[117].

And interesting to note the number of the twelve city gates, placed in groups of three on each side which correspond to one of the cardinal point: this distribution puts off that of the stones in the breastplate, in groups of three, on four horizontal rows[118].

As the breastplate worn by the high priest, the heavenly Jerusalem has a square shape[119] and it is adorned with twelve precious gems. The holy city is the bride finally consecrated to God, which makes it shining of his glory, while the size of the city is determined by a high wall, in which there are 'twelve gates' to indicate the tribes of Israel, by which every nation has access to the city. Although in a different order, Book of Revelation 21 mentions the twelve stones that form the foundations of the city of God, the symbol of the twelve apostles that form the new Israel, the Church. However, the here cited stones do not match all to the twelve minerals in Exodus 28. If one compares the two series, one notes that only nine stones are cited in both books: jasper, sapphire, emerald, carnelian, chrysolite, beryl, topaz, hyacinth, and amethyst; therefore, in Revelation the ruby (or turquoise, according to the biblical version), agate and onyx are not mentioned.

---

116 Rev 21,9-27.

117 Ezek 48,30-35.

118 The same pattern can be found in the distribution of the apostles in the *Last Supper* of Leonardo.

119 According to the Jewish myth, in the fourth heaven, Zebul, there are the heavenly Jerusalem, the temple and the altar (R. Graves, R. Patai, *I Miti ebraici*, tit. or. *Hebrew Miths*, Milano 1969, v. 18).

According to Father La Grua, the ruby (nophek) was also translated 'carbunculus', 'anthrax', from the Latin Vulgate[120], but could also be called karchedon[121] (from the greek name of Carthage), or 'chalcedony', stone cited in Revelation[122]. There is in fact a reddish variety of chalcedony, a silicon dioxide containing iron; this is confirmed by Pliny, who distinguished between two types of carbuncles, one 'male' more intense color, and a 'female', more rosy hue[123]. In the variety sky-blue, chalcedony it was probably confused with turquoise mentioned in Exodus[124] and is associated with the tribe of Judah. The seventh stone, in Hebrew leshem, could be identified with hyacinth. Finally, the aforementioned agate Exodus could be identified with the chrysoprase (the tenth stone described in the book) or with sardonyx, a variety of onyx also belonging to the genus 'chalcedony'[125].

Esodo *Exodus*	Ezechiele *Ezekiel*	LXX	Vulgata
Odhem	Odhem	Sardion	Sardius
Pit'dah (o piteda)	Pit'dah (o piteda)	Topation	Topatius
Bareket	Bareket	Smaragdos	Smaragdus
Nophek (o nofek)	Nophek (o nofek)	Anthrax	Carbunculus
Sappyir (o sappir)	Sappyir (o sappir)	Saphiros	Sapphirus
Yahalom (o Jahalon)	Yahalom (o Jahalon)	Jaspis	Jaspis
Lesham (o lesem)	-	Ligurion	Ligurius
Shebuw (o sebo)	-	Achates	Achates
Ahlamah (o achlama)	-	Amethystos	Amethistus
Tarsis (o tarshish)	Tarsis (o tarshish)	Chrysolithos	Chrysolithus
Soham (o shoham)	Soham (o shoham)	Beryllos	Onychinus
Yashfeh (o Jaspeh)	Yashfeh (o Jaspeh)	Onychion	Beryllus

120 The Latin Vulgate was used till the XX century.
121 C. Plinio, cit., XXXVII, 32.
122 M. G. La Grua, *Cristo nelle pietre preziose,* cit., p. 34.
123 C. Plinio, cit., XXXVII, 32.
124 Ex 28,15-21; Ex 39,8-21 (Version CEI-Gerusalemme).
125 Five of the twelve stones cited in *Rev* 21 belong to the genus 'chalcedony': jasper, agate, onix, carnelian, chrysoprase. I thank prof. Franco Maria Boschetto for this information.

Symbology of the stones in the Middle Ages

Even the Middle Ages gave the stones a strong symbolic value; virtues, characteristics and colour of the gems have been known since ancient times[126]. Already in late antiquity, Bishop Severian of Gabala (d. after 408), listed a number of minerals in a sermon attributed to him and he associated a stone to each apostle, but with a different order: anthrax to Thomas, the emerald to Simon the Zealot, the crystal (diamond) to Thaddeus, agate to Judas of James, chalcedony to Judas Iscariot, the Sardinian to Peter, the beryl to Andrew, amethyst to John, hyacinth to James of Zebedee, the topaz to Matthew, the hyacinth James of Alpheus and the pearl to Philip[127]. Middle Ages associated minerals to Christian symbols and allegories considered stones of angels, saints, patriarchs and apostles[128]. For example, Isidore of Seville (ca. 560 - 636) identified the nine angelic choirs in the nine stones cited by Ezekiel, in which he recognized the virtues of the devil before his fall[129]. Other authors instead focused their attention on the *Book of Revelation*; between the various comments to the text of John, the *Commentary on the Apocalypse* of the Venerable Bede (673-735) was important, a Benedictine friar and Doctor of the Church, who wrote it around 709. In addition to the fundamental text of Bede, also the *Moral Commentary Job of Gregory the Great* and his *commentary on Revelation* of Haimo of Auxerre provided the Middle Ages with the theological interpretations of gems[130]. As the Church, the new Israel, celebrates the sacrifice of Christ on the altar, new and eternal Priest, since the early Middle Ages the gems were used to decorate altars and liturgical furnishings (chalices, patens, votive crosses, robes, etc.). The objects of worship were embellished with seven stones indicating the gifts of the Holy Spirit: the diamond (the fortress), sapphire (wisdom), ruby (devotion), topaz (knowledge), emerald (understanding), amethyst (good advice), chalcedony (fear of God)[131]. In the Middle Ages, stones were used to create amulets that were believed to have magical powers, worn to protect against adverse spirits and to ensure the health of body and soul. Who told us about the virtues of precious stones, are the *Lapidaries*, educational-scientific literary works describing the minerals according to classical and oriental traditions, which indicate

---

126 A. Lipinsky, *Oro, argento,* cit., pp. 277-387; G. Devoto, A. Molayem, *Archeogemmologia: pietre antiche, glittica, magia e litoterapia,* Roma 1990.

127 D. Righi, *Una omelia sugli apostoli attribuita a Severiano di Gabala,* 1995, pubbl. 2004, vol. 1, pp. 86 e 102.

128 E. Schoonhoven, *Fra Dio e l'imperatore: il simbolismo delle pietre preziose nella Divina Commedia,* in *Dante, rivista internazionale di studi su Dante Alighieri,* voll. 3 e 4, Pisa – Roma 2006, p. 74.

129 A. Carpin, *Angeli e demòni nella sintesi patristica di Isidoro di Siviglia,* Bologna 2004, p.90; Isidorus, *Sententiae,* I 10, 15: CCL 111, 34; cf. PL 83, 556; by G. S. Abbolito, Venerabile Beda, *Omelie sul Vangelo.* Roma 1990.

130 E. Schoonhoven, *Fra Dio e l'imperatore,* cit., p. 79.

131 A. M. Tripputi, *PGR, Per grazia ricevuta,* vol. 1, Bari 2002, p. 108.

the healing properties and apotropaic virtues. According to Rivière, the medieval *Lapidaries* were inspired by the heavenly city described in *Revelation* 21[132]. Among many in circulation, the more considered was the *Liber de seu lapidum gemmis* by Marbod bishop of Rennes (1035-1123), perhaps dating back to a Greek text by Damieron from the first century[133].

The successive treaties derived from Marbod, such as the *De Mineralibus*, composed in 1260 by the Bishop of Regensburg Albertus Magnus (ca. 1193 -1280) and *L'intelligenza* (late XIII - early XIV c.), a ninth rhyme poem by an unknown author, attributed to Dino Compagni and in which the minerals are described in the order in which they appear in the *Lapidary* of Cecco d'Ascoli.

In the *Book of Gems* by Hildegard of Bingen (1098-1179), she says about the stones:

> *Despite their use befitting in many situations, they can not be applied except with good and honest intentions, and therefore they can not profit in works of seduction, fornication, adultery, murder, actions which are dictated by enmity and related circumstances, which reflect the vices and they are contrary to the human character; the very nature of the stones claims a fair and appropriate behaviour, and shuns the evil and perverse conduct of men... God had honored the first angel (Lucifer) of the most dazzling jewels... Then his mind became hubris, for the splendour of stones he wore, was reflected in God; He convinced himself he could realize equal if not superior businesses to God's purposes, and therefore its brightness faded... but God did not allow the splendour of gems and their properties got lost, but he wanted them to be honoured and sacred on ground and used for medicinal purposes[134].*

According to Hildegard, the devil avoids the stones, because they remind him of his former glory. The reference is to the accusations against the king of Tyre in the *Book of Ezekiel*, who was lifted up by the accumulated wealth, up to believe himself a 'god'. The text reveals behind this individual a very different 'angelic' figure:

> *Moreover the word of the Lord came to me, saying, «Son of man, take up a lamentation for the king of Tyre, and say to him, thus says the Lord God: You were the seal of perfection, full of wisdom and perfect in beauty. You were in Eden, the garden of God; every precious stone was your covering: the sardius, topaz, and diamond, beryl, onyx, and jasper, sapphire, turquoise, and emerald with gold. The workmanship of your timbrels and pipes was prepared for you on the day you were created. You were the anointed cherub who covers; I established you; you were on the holy mountain of God; You walked back and forth in the midst of fiery stones. You were perfect in your ways from the day you were created, till iniquity was found in you. By the abundance of your trading you became filled with violence within, and you sinned; therefore I cast you as a profane thing out of the mountain of God; And I destroyed you, o covering cherub, from the midst of the fiery*

---

132 J. M. Rivière, *Amuleti Talismani e Pantacoli*, cit., pp. 239-240.
133 treccani.it/enciclopedia/lapidario_(Enciclopedia-Italiana)/(last visit: 28.08.2016).
134 Ildegarda di Bingen, Marbodo di Rennes, *Il libro delle gemme*, Torino 1998, pp. 18-19.

stones. Your heart was lifted up because of your beauty; you corrupted your wisdom for the sake of your splendor; I cast you to the ground, I laid you before kings, that they might gaze at you. You defiled your sanctuaries by the multitude of your iniquities, by the iniquity of your trading; therefore I brought fire from your midst. It devoured you, and I turned you to ashes upon the earth in the sight of all who saw you. All who knew you among the peoples are astonished at you; you have become a horror, and shall be no more forever. The word of the Lord came to me: «Son of man, set your face towards Sidon, and prophesy against her and say, Thus says the Lord God: Behold, I am against you, O Sidon, and I will manifest my glory in your midst. And they shall know that I am the Lord when I execute judgements in her and manifest my holiness in her [135].

Similarly, to the tribe-stone relationship, with the exception of Judas, the Middle Ages attributed to every apostle a mineral [136].

One of those days Jesus went out to a mountainside to pray, and spent the night praying to God. When morning came, he called his disciples to him and chose twelve of them, whom he also designated apostles: Simon (whom he named Peter), his brother Andrew, James, John, Philip, Bartholomew, Matthew, Thomas, James son of Alphaeus, Simon who was called the Zealot, Judas son of James, and Judas Iscariot, who became a traitor [137].

As one can notice, the *Book of Revelation* mentions the twelve stones with another order with respect to the *Exodus*. The association went forming with respect to the order of the disciple's call, and to the order in which every stone is mentioned in *Revelation* 21 (see next diagram).

---

135 Ezek 28,11-22.
136 G. B. Ladner, *Il simbolismo paleocristiano,* cit., Milano 2008, p. 153.
137 Lk 6,12-16.

Thus the following relationships had gone forming:

The 12 Foundations	Stone	Apostle
I Foundation	Jasper	Simon Peter
II Foundation	Sapphire	Andrew
III Foundation	Chalcedony (agate)	James the Elder
IV Foundation	Emerald	John
V Foundation	Sardonyx (onix)	Philip
VI Foundation	Carnelian	Bartholomew
VII Foundation	Beryl (or crysolite)	Matthew
VIII Foundation	Beryl (green quality)	Thomas
IX Foundation	Topaz	James the Lesser
X Foundation	Chrysoprasus	Thaddeus (Jude)
XI Foundation	Hyacinth	Simon the Canaanite
XII Foundation	Amethyst	Matthias

First foundation: Jasper.

Hildegard of Bingen believed jasper was useful against one ear deafness, against colds, infections, nightmares and hallucinations, as well as it was able to purify the air from the influence of evil spirits. It profited also the woman who had just given birth to a son, and it healed the bites of snakes[138]. According to Cecco d'Ascoli (1269-1327), the mineral 'was born by the power of Mars, by a mixture of varied and many colours; it mitigates and lets the virtues in us secure. In the great issues, it makes the man confident'. Moreover, Cecco believed that the stone favoured chastity and that the warriors had to bring it 'tied in silver'[139].

Even Dino Compagni, describing the magical powers of sixty stones set in the crown of a statue of the Madonna, stated that the green jasper manifests its virtues on a silver frame, it profited to the pain of childbirth and 'who wears it, in his defence, drives out ghosts and destroys fevers. In addition, by wearing it when it is consecrated, it makes the person powerful and honoured, pleasing to arrive in great honour'[140]. The medieval tradition has associated the first foundation of the Heavenly City to the Petrine primacy. Despite being regarded as a comparison to other low-value stone, jasper was not far behind in the virtues. Probably the tradition relates the chromatic variety of the gemstone to the many virtues of the apostle: Peter was the first to enter the empty tomb and to preach on the day of Pentecost; the first who converted Jews and Gentiles, the first to confess Christ publicly:

> Now when Jesus came into the district of Caesarea Philippi, he asked his disciples, «Who do people say that the Son of Man is?» And they said, «Some say John the Baptist, others say Elijah, and others Jeremiah or one of the prophets». He said to them, «But who do you say that I am?» Simon Peter replied, «You are the Christ, the Son of the living God». And Jesus answered him, «Blessed are you, Simon Bar-Jonah! For flesh and blood has not revealed this to you, but my Father who is in heaven. And I tell you, you are Peter, and on this rock I will build my church, and the gates of hell shall not prevail against it. I will give you the keys of the kingdom of heaven, and whatever you bind on earth shall be bound in heaven, and whatever you loose on earth shall be loosed in heaven». Then he strictly charged the disciples to tell no one that he was the Christ[141].

---

138 *Il libro delle gemme*, cit., p. 38.
139 Cecco d'Ascoli, *L'acerba*, by C. Crespi, Ascoli Piceno 1927, III, XVII, vv. 15-16
140 D. Compagni, *L'intelligenza*, Milano 1863, pp. 8-9.
141 Mt 16,13-20.

Second Foundation: Sapphire

By virtue of its color, the Middle Ages believed the sapphire was a spiritual rock that could drive a person closer to God, to the extent that St. Albert the Great in his treatise *De mineralibus* said 'if you want to achieve peace, take the oriental sapphire, because it creates harmony and makes the man devoted to God'[142]. Hildegard indicated it as to hunt the spirits and calm the fire of passion, to wake the intelligence and healing blurred vision[143], while according to Marbod, if it was mixed with milk, it brought healing to all plagues[144]. Symbol of security, it was set in engagement rings (the Lombard sovereigns Theodelinda and Agilulfo sanctioned their engagement by drinking from the same cup of sapphire). About the stone, Cecco d'Ascoli wrote:

> By Jupiter's power, it comforts the heart, said the eastern, serve the limbs and powers their virtue; it works against fever, poison and anthrax, if it is used immediately onthe evil; it comforts the face and preserves peace; tt takes away the malignant envy from the heart, it flees the fear and makes the man bold, the woman humble and it designates chastity[145].

Sapphire is also quoted in *L'intelligenza* by Dino Compagni:

> Gem of the other gems, dear and beautiful, it preserves the virtue that has not collapsed. It maintains people humble and with good-aire, and it is of value in necromancy. It presents the Virgin Lady in her height, with her clarity shining over heaven[146].

The Middle Ages associated to Andrew, Peter's brother, the gem that lit eyes and body with the properties of light[147], requirement of God himself. Andrew took part to the call of the other apostles, and he evangelised Asia Minor, Russia and Greece[148].

---

142 B. Alberti Magni, *Opera omnia,* Parisiis Apud Ludovicum Vivès, 1890, v. 5, II-II, p. 16 s.
143 *Il libro delle gemme,* cit., p. 29.
144 *Il libro delle gemme,* cit., p. 163.
145 Cecco d'Ascoli, *L'acerba,* cit., III, XVI, v. 37- 45.
146 D. Compagni, *L'intelligenza,* cit., p. 9.
147 *Il libro delle gemme,* cit., p. 63.
148 santiebeati.it/dettaglio/22000 (last visit 22.08.2016).

Third Foundation: Chalcedony

The chalcedony was held in high regard too. Hildegard thought it was able to dispel the weaknes-ses of man, it gave expressive force and if placed on the skin, it had the power to energize the body[149]. The author of *L'Intelligenza* believed chalcedony made of 'the color of hyacinth and beryl: for his virtue, it flees the demon, distancing him away and keeping him in torment'[150]. St. Albert the Great thought that chalcedony was able to ward off melancholy, and wrote his own experiences on the use of stone[151].

As among the various types there is also the reddish variety, as it has been mentioned, in ancient times the term *charchedon*, deriving perhaps from *Karchedon* (Carthage) indicated both the chalcedony[152] and the anthrax, so much so that the two stones were associated to the same mineral[153]. Since it was associated to the sacrifice of Christ like the ruby, anthrax was worn as a sign of protection. A mineral that was 'red over any clear and beautiful stone'[154], and together with chalcedony, it was considered able to ward off the spirits[155]. However, since agate belongs to the genre of chalcedony too, it is difficult to tell which was the aforementioned stone in *Revelation* 21. As regards as the powers of the stone, similarly to Pliny, Hildegard of Bingen believed the agate was a good remedy against poisonous insects' bites, because it was able to absorb the poison[156], while Marbod of Rennes considered it effective against the viper bite and skin diseases [157]. Hildegard still considered it a stone capable of giving force (it was worn by athletes to be invincible), used to cure epilepsy and convulsions, to give wisdom and reason to those who wore constantly, and it was also able to ward off the thieves from one's home[158]. Cecco d'Ascoli also recognized the power to benefit the eyes, to donate the discretion of the word and win battles. Brought to the mouth, it removed thirst and, as noted by the author of the *Acerba*, 'it makes the man handsome in human views'[159], while Comrades writes 'virginity seems to be its

---

149 *Il libro delle gemme*, cit., p. 39.
150 D. Compagni, *L'intelligenza*, cit., p. 9.
151 *De mineralibus*, II, tr. 2, c. 3, *chalcedonius*, ed. Borgnet 5, 33°, p. 78, English translation by D. Wyckoff, *Book of Minerals*, Oxford 1967.
152 C. Plinio, cit., XXXVII, 35.
153 M. La Grua, *Cristo nelle pietre preziose*, cit., pp. 34-35.
154 D. Compagni, *L'intelligenza*, cit., p. 14.
155 *Il libro delle gemme*, cit., p. 43.
156 *Il libro delle gemme*, cit., p. 45.
157 *Il libro delle gemme*, cit., p. 60.
158 *Il libro delle gemme*, cit., p. 44-45.
159 Cecco d'Ascoli, *L'acerba*, cit., III, XVI, vv. 75-77.

delight, and gives virtues to many infirmities, snakes and it chases 'vain enchantments'[160].

Chalcedony, III foundation of the Heavenly City, is referred to James of Zebedee (the Major). First martyr among the apostles, the love of Christ led him to show himself strong in persecutions. And since union property is proper of love, James joined to Christ to bring all his will to that of the Master, just like the mineral that in the old mindset, held to the light of the Sun and the ardor of the fire. Nicknamed with his brother John *Boanerges*, 'sons of thunder', he evan-gelized Spain. He was beheaded in Jerusalem around the year 44 by order of Herod Agrippa[161].

160 D. Compagni, *L'intelligenza,* cit., p. 8.
161 santiebeati.it/dettaglio/21250 (last visit 22.08.2016).

Fourth Foundation: Emerald

Emeralds were much acclaimed stones in ancient times and widely used[162]. Hildegard of Bingen believed them to be formed in rocks at sunrise when vegetation awakens[163]. Among the various virtues, Rennes Marbod believed them capable of making people eloquent, improving sight and aiding recovery from fever. He also associated them with knowledge of secret things, prosperity, purity, love and respect[164]. On the subject of emeralds, Cecco d'Ascoli has observed:

Mercurio è che spira sua virtute, nello smeraldo ch'è sopra ogni verde; di molte infirmitati fa salute... conforta la memoria e la natura, gli spirti fuga e loro false scorte. Chi vuole divinar seco lo porte[165].

Mercury inspires the power of the emerald, whose green is better of every green. It heals many diseases... comforting memory and human nature, scares away the spirits and their bad friends. Those who want to predict the future, bring the emerald that gives divine inspiration.

For Dino Compagni, 'lo smeraldo verde ha vertude in crescer le ricchezze' (green emerald has virtue to increasing wealth)[166]. Jacopo da Varazze's comments in the *Genoa Chronicle* are also interesting: during the First Crusade, taking part in the 1101 capture of Caesarea, Genoese soldiers under the command of Guglielmo Embriaco found the bowl that Jesus ate the *Last Supper* from and Nicodemus used to collect the blood of the Lord[167]. If it is true, on one hand, that the author expresses no opinion as to the authenticity of the relic, thus leaving various possibilities open, on the other hand the same information is reported by Iacopo Doria in a footnote to *Liber Liberatione civitatum Orientis* by Caffaro[168]. Known as the 'Holy Basin' and thought to be emerald, the relic became part of the San Lorenzo Cathedral in Genoa's treasures where it is still kept. A century later, Wolfram von Eschenbach (1170 ca.-1220 ca.), knight, and perhaps Templar[169]drew on the French versions of Chrétien de Troyes and a mysterious Kyot de Provence, between 1200

---

162 A. Teifascite, *Fior di pensieri sulle Pietre Preziose,* translation by A. Raineri, Firenze 1818 , vol. 1, p. 18.

163 *Il libro delle gemme,* cit., p. 20.

164 *Il libro delle gemme,* cit., p. 65.

165 Cecco d'Ascoli, *L'acerba,* cit., III, XVI, v. 55-62.

166 D. Compagni, *L'intelligenza,* cit., p.8.

167 *Iacopo da Varagine e la sua Cronaca di Genova dalle origini al MCCXCVII*: v. 2. Cronaca, Tipografia del Senato, Roma 1941, pp. 222-223 e 279-280.

168 D. Calcagno, *Il Sacro catino, specchio dell'identità genovese,* in *Xenia antiqua,* Roma 2001, vol. 10, p. 44 s.

169 A. Romano, *Federico II legislatore del Regno di Sicilia nell'Europa del Duecento: per una storia comparata delle codificazioni europee,* atti del convegno internazionale di studi per le celebrazioni dell'VIII Centenario della Nascita di Federico II, Messina-Reggio Calabria 1995, p. 565.

and 1210[170], and wrote the Arthurian romance *Parzival*[171]. Thanks to Arab manuscripts found in Toledo, Kiot would later in turn become aware of the 'Grail-emerald relationship'. In the texts we read of a certain Flegetanis, from King Solomon's line, who read in the stars of an object called 'Grail', carried by angels on the Earth and since then kept by pure men[172] reporting that the emerald-Grail broke off from Lucifer's crown (or the front) during conflict or when he rushed into hell. As described, for the prerogative of virginity, the Middle Ages associated John to the emerald, a symbol of heavenly hope. With regard to *Revelation* written by John, the stone was also believed to be able to reveal things to come and to donate effective words to persuade[173], the youth and vigor of the tree of the cross were associated to, similarly to John, who kept intact the faith under the cross, before the most terrible torments of the Master. In the *Golden Legend*, Jacopo da Varazze described John as a young man whose name refers to the grace of its virginal state, and he highlighted the special love from the Lord to him:

> *For Christ loved him more than the other apostles and showed more signs of affection and friendship to him, as 'God's grace' means 'pleasing to the Lord'. The second privilege is the integrity of the flesh, because the Lord wanted him virgin; the third privilege is the revelation of the secret, and therefore it is said: the one to whom it was given; In fact, he had the gift of knowing many deep secrets like those on the divinity of the Word and the end of the world. The fourth privilege is that he was entrusted with the mother of God[174]. Together with the women of Jerusalem, John was one of the first witnesses of the Resurrection and he had always represented the perfect disciple of Jesus, the follower who was able to participate in the events of the Master up to experience himself the reality of the empty tomb and to recognize the risen Lord on sthe ea of Galilee: 'the disciple whom Jesus loved said to Peter, «it is the Lord»[175].*

170 On *Parsifal*, C. Grünanger, in *Storia della letteratura tedesca. Il Medioevo,* Milano, 1955; W. Deinert, *Ritter und Kosmos in Parzival,* Monaco, 1960; H. Kratz, *Wolframs Parzival. An Attempt at a Total Evaluation,* Berna, 1973; G. de Montreuil, *Perceval,* Milano, 1986; treccani.it / enciclopedia / wolfram-von-eschenbach / (last visit: 21.08.2016).

171 Masterpiece of medieval German literature, the story of the *Grail* cycle is a wise Legend, in which Eschenbach refers explicitly to an Islamic source.

172 A. Romano, *Federico II legislatore del Regno di Sicilia,* cit., p. 565.

173 *Il libro delle gemme,* cit., p. 65.

174 Jacopo da Varazze, *Legenda Aurea*, trans. from Latin by di G. P. Maggioni, Firenze 2007, p. 103.

175 John 21,7.

Fifth Foundation: Onyx

This stone was recommended to be quick in the talks and to end the conflicts, to heal abdominal colic and the bites of spiders and scorpions. Hildegard considered it effective in cardiac and respiratory disturbances, stomach disorders, weak spleen and eyesight, and to treat anxiety[176].

The genre 'Chalcedony' is defined by Cecco d'Ascoli:

Pale and colorless; of youth it preserves the destinations, with virtue, it wins trouble and values. If it is punctured, it resists even better evil spirits and their mockery[177].

Similarly, Compagni wrote about onyx that 'the virtue for it was established, the images and dreams hunt away'[178]. The sardonyx is instead a chalcedony composed of Sardinian and onyx, from which it differs for the darker and reddish bands. Teifascite remembered different qualities, such as the one made up of red and white layers, and the one of whites and blacks layers. While recognizing the power of the stone in benefitting childbirth[179], it was nicknamed gieza, 'sadness', because of anxiety, moodiness and bad dreams caused to those who wore it around the neck or hands, so much that it was avoided in kings' treasures[180]. The medieval tradition associated it to the figure of Philip, pure heart apostle.

Man of upright conscience and of great faith, he was ready to talk about Christ to Nathanael, and he did not hesitate to follow the Lord when he called him to follow him. He received the Holy Spirit, he brought the Gospel in Scythia, where he founded a Christian community. Subsequently, he went to Phrygia[181], where he attracted many to the faith, to the point of attracting the hatred of the idolaters. Philip was martyred at eighty-four, dying stoned to death or nailed to a tree upside down[182]. According to the tradition, as onyx restored eyes to an optimal view, so Philip had the bright look that he always kept in God: while the other apostles asked Christ to become great, Philip asked to see the Father's face:

---

176 *Il libro delle gemme,* cit., pp. 24-25.
177 Cecco d'Ascoli, *L'acerba,* cit., III, XVI, vv. 68- 72.
178 D. Compagni, *L'intelligenza,* cit., p.10.
179 Teifascite brings a tale of Armenusio Antioch, according to whom the onyx was wrapped the hair of pregnant women to favor immediate deliver, *Fior di pensieri sulle Pietre Preziose,* cit., vol. 1, p. 47.
180 A. Teifascite, *Fior di pensieri sulle Pietre Preziose,* vol. 1, pp. 46-47.
181 Jacopo da Varazze, *Legenda aurea,* cit., pp. 1548-1549.
182 santodelgiorno.it/santi-filippo-e-giacomo/(last visit 22.08.16).

Jesus said to him, «I am the way, and the truth, and the life. No one comes to the Father except through me. If you had known me, you would have known my Father also. From now on you do know him and have seen him». Philip said to him, «Lord, show us the Father, and it is enough for us.» Jesus said to him, «Have I been with you so long, and you still do not know me, Philip? Whoever has seen me has seen the Father. How can you say, 'Show us the Father'? Do you not believe that I am in the Father and the Father is in me? The words that I say to you I do not speak on my own authority, but the Father who dwells in me does his works. Believe me that I am in the Father and the Father is in me, or else believe on account of the works themselves. Truly, truly, I say to you, whoever believes in me will also do the works that I do; and greater works than these will he do, because I am going to the Father. Whatever you ask in my name, this I will do, that the Father may be glorified in the Son. If you ask me anything in my name, I will do it»[183].

183 John 14,6-14.

Sixth Foundation: Carnelian

Of the carnelian, Cecco d'Ascoli, similarly to the ancients, wrote that 'it squeezes blood for the virtues that it inspires'; equally Hildegard and St. Albert the Great considered it capable of stopping bleeding in case of deep wounds[184].

The Middle Ages effectively associated the carnelian to Bartholomew, who died skinned alive[185]. Because of his martyrdom, the tradition associated to him the contempt of his garments, and he is often depicted in art with his skin in his hand.

We know that the carnelian was confused with ruby and garnet, about which the author of *Acerba* wrote that 'in him it is great perfection that comforts us in all our nature from us removing the suspect'[186]. Associated to blood pouring, the ruby was considered worthy of heaven, as the stone was dedicated to delight the divine view. Since the tradition believed precisely that the angels had the power to bind demons, Bartholomew was considered a great saint[187]: we know that having to preach the Gospel in Lycaonia (current Cappadocia) and India, after having conquered the idolatry, he went to Armenia, where he healed the sick and lame people, made so by the worship of idols[188].

184 Cecco d'Ascoli, *L'acerba,* cit., III, XVIII, v.122; *Il libro delle gemme,* cit., p. 55; Alberto Magno, *De mineralibus,* II, tr. 2, c. 3, *cornelius,* pp. 81-82.
185 santiebeati.it/dettaglio/21400 (last visit: 22.08.2106).
186 Cecco d'Ascoli, *L'acerba,* cit., III, XVII, v. 72- 74.
187 santodelgiorno.it/san-bartolomeo/ (last visit: 22.08.2106).
188 santiebeati.it/dettaglio/21400 (last visit: 22.08.2106).

Seventh Foundation: Chrysolite

This stone was considered a powerful amulet. Hildegard of Bingen considered it capable of giving life energy, to calm fever, heart pains and, similarly to Marbod of Rennes, able to remove the anguishes and the air spirits[189]. The author of *L'Intelligenza* talked about it as a resplendent aura, 'the night drives out and destroys fears, and the enemy flees for his virtue'[190]. St. Albert the Great also cited the chrysolite in his *Lapidary*, considering it a stone able to grant wisdom[191]. The chrysolite is associated to the publican who, with a simple nod by the Redeemer, abandoned the usury counter and began to follow him living in poverty. Matthew, who is the one among the apostles who reminds of worldly happiness, is related to the stone where the beauty of gold glitters, because after the conversion he sought gold in the evangelical wisdom scorning what he had loved before and multiplying the zeal towards God. After the meeting with the lord, in the Gospel he cited these words of Jesus:

> *So when you give to the needy, do not announce it with trumpets, as the hypocrites do in the synagogues and on the streets, to be honored by others. Truly I tell you, they have received their reward in full. But when you give to the needy, do not let your left hand know what your right hand is doing, so that your giving may be in secret. Then your Father, who sees what is done in secret, will reward you[192].*

By virtue of his conversion, Levi Matthew was considered the truest example for sinners, urged not to despair of salvation, but as Zacchaeus, to give back four times the defrauded money[193].

---

189 *Il libro delle gemme,* cit., p. 36 e 67.
190 D. Compagni, *L'intelligenza,* cit., p. 10.
191 *De mineralibus,* II, tr. 2, c. 3, *chrysolitus,* cit., p. 82.
192 Mt 6,2-4.
193 Lk 19,1-10.

Eighth Foundation: Beryl

Beryl was often confused with diamond, reference to the same figure of the Church[194]. Regarded in the Middle Ages among the most valuable stones, beryl was perhaps imported from India if it is true what the author of *L'Intelligenza* reported: 'the first stone that was found in parts of India'[195]. It was believed to be able to stop the backbiting and to dominate the language, as well as to hold off the demon, to the extent that wearing it meant to be invincible[196]. As mentioned, beryl was easily confused with diamond, about whom Cecco d'Ascoli wrote:

Neither for fire nor for iron the diamond breaks for Saturn's power, it resists its nature to necromancer. It chases off the spirits, toxic and fear. It lights up love if disdain is in charge[197].

As it has been said, what adorned the breastplate was beryl, a stone that if brought with oneself, it protected from the wrath, it benefited the liver and lovers exchange it as a sign of loyalty, because 'for its virtue it makes love grow'[198]. This mineral, 'pale green, similar to an emerald', relieved sighs, resisted the enemy, kept the liver and stomach healthy, gave a keen intellect, benefit the wedding and made 'increases mind faculties towards the enemies'[199].

Beryl is related to the figure of Thomas, the apostle who asked the Lord to put his hands onto his breast to prove him risen[200]. Because of its pale green colour, beryl was associated with the inconstancy of faith while, as regards the name Thomas, Jacopo da Varazze among the various possible meanings reports *totus means*, meaning the ability to enter totally in God's love and contemplation[201]. Particularly hard stone, beryl was also related to the apostle because of his obstinacy, because 'believing' and 'seeing' are opposed to each other, and the faith that needs proof is not really such.

---

194 S. Cavenago-Bignami, *Gemmologia*, cit., p. 171.
195 D. Compagni, *L'intelligenza*, cit., p. 8.
196 *Il libro delle gemme*, cit., p. 26.
197 Cecco d'Ascoli, *L'acerba*, cit, III, XVI, v. 13- 17.
198 D. Compagni, *L'intelligenza*, cit., p. 11.
199 Cecco d'Ascoli, *L'acerba*, cit., III, XVI, v. 96-104.
200 John 20,24-29.
201 Jacopo da Varazze, *Legenda Aurea*, cit., p. 63.

Ninth Foundation: Topaz

The Middle Ages believed that the topaz won the fury of the sea while traveling by ship[202], it assured business in trades and prevented the risk of poisoning. Dipped in wine, it was thought it would guarantee a good view, depart nervousness, fever, leprosy and spleen pain. In addition, it protected by asthma, by bleeding, insomnia, and it donated inner peace[203]. Cecco d'Ascoli exalted it as sunstone: it resists 'anger, sadness and bustle', it gives dignity and 'over every stone it shows clarity[204]. Its brilliance earned him the motto 'Gemma fulgidior omni'[205]. Linked to the values of boldness and creativity, it was connected to the Sun and the sign of Leo.

The tradition associates the ninth foundation of the Heavenly City to James said 'the Minor', to distinguish him from James of Zebedee, brother of John. Probably he was one of the cousins of Christ from his father's side (Alfeo-Cleophas was the brother of St. Joseph). He was the first bishop of Jerusalem, after the martyrdom of James the Greater in the year 42 and he wrote a letter to the Christians of Jewish origins urging them to hope and charity. Nicknamed 'The right among the apostles' for the integrity of his life[206], James died victim of Jewish fanaticism[207]. Giuseppe Flavio writes:

Anano [...] summoned the judges of the Sanhedrin and introduced before them a man named James, Jesus' brother, who was surnamed Christ, and certain others, on charges of having transgressed the law, and he delivered them to be stoned[208].

202 *Il libro delle gemme,* cit., p. 68.
203 *Il libro delle gemme,* cit., p. 33-35.
204 Cecco d'Ascoli, *L'acerba,* cit., III, XVII, v. 10-12.
205 P. Polo, *Mansiones Festaque Hebraeorum: Literaliter Descripta Moraliter, Mistice*, Barcellona 1725, tomo I, LIX, XXXVII, p. 201.
206 santodelgiorno.it/santi-filippo-e-giacomo/(last visit: 22.07.16)
    it.cathopedia.org/wiki/San_Giacomo_il_Minore (last visit: 22.07.2016).
207 G. Caldarelli, *Atti dei martiri,* Milano 1996, p. 56.
208 Giuseppe Flavio, *Antichità giudaiche*, XX, 200.

James was stoned to death in the year 61 or 62, during a popular revolt instigated by the high priest Hanan. Since the topaz was considered among the most precious stones in the world, to the extent that it could not be compared to others – it was well associated to the apostle James, whose tradition attributed the values of the fortress, honour and decorum. His life was a mirror of virtue and holiness: with a face similar to that of Christ, James also resembled to him in soul and love. The topaz was therefore associated with James for the preciousness of its light and the perfect imitation of Christ. Perhaps that is why the tradition believed the apostle was worthy to enter the Holy of Holies, where the high priest could enter only once a year; however, it is unlikely that this was true, since James belonged to the tribe of Judah as Christ, and the priesthood was the prerogative of the Levites.

Tenth Foundation: Chrysoprase

Variety of chalcedony, varying from green to blue-green, in the Middle Ages the chrysoprase was used in event of gout and seizures. It was then thought it reduced selfishness and anger, and favoured attention and imagination. It benefits the eyes, and because it was believed that the devil hated holy water, it was useful to cast out demons from the body and to reach the emotional balance[209]. The tradition associates the tenth foundation of the heavenly Jerusalem, made of chrysoprase, to the brother of James, Jude said 'Thaddeus', 'magnanimous'. The *Gospel of John* mentions him in relation to the *Last Supper* of Jesus, when Thaddeus asks Jesus:

> *Then Judas (not Judas Iscariot) said, «But, Lord, why do you intend to show yourself to us and not to the world?» Jesus replied, «Anyone who loves me will obey my teaching. My Father will love them, and we will come to them and make our home with them»[210].*

After the Ascension, Judas Thaddaeus dedicates himself to proclaiming the Gospel, bringing the light of Christ to the pagans. Perhaps, he died a martyr and was buried in Persia. Apostle of living faith, firm hope and ardent charity, he is traditionally called for desperate causes. The property of chrysoprase to benefit the view was compared to the Holy authority to heal the weakness of the eyes of the mind, and as the gem shines in the darkness, so the green-gold colour is related to the desire for holiness of Thaddeus, shining during the tribulations for the propagation of the Gospel. As the gem benefit against the disease of leprosy and purified the heart from the greed of wealth, so Thaddeus, pure-hearted and magnanimous apostle, was effective against the disease of vices.

---

209 *Il libro delle gemme,* cit., pp. 40-41.
210 John 14,22-23.

Eleventh Foundation: Jacinth

Marbod Rennes distinguished three varieties of hyacinth of different colour: pomegranate (most valuable), cedar and sea-green.

Since if exposed to fire, it becomes white, in the Middle Ages it was taken as a symbol of faith, courage and resourcefulness, and also because it was believed to reassure those who were traveling to a foreign land. It was believed it would enhance mental abilities, benefit the stomach and it would increase the appetite, it would reconcile sleep and solve the blurred vision[211]. Hildegard of Bingen considered it useful in case of foolishness' possession, to hunt the spirits, especially associated with the recitation of this formula:

God, who deprived the demon of his precious stones because he had transgressed its provisions, keep away from (name) every demon and spell and free you from the pain of this madness[212].

Among the many varieties, the author recalls the red hyacinth, of a beautiful and vivid colour, considered the most valuable and expensive. The medieval tradition related the eleventh hyacinth base to Simon the Zealot[213], apostle connected to the rioters group that was a big political and military problem for Rome. The news on this apostle are scarce; according to tradition, he suffered a terrible martyrdom, being torn to pieces with a saw.

---

211 *Il libro delle gemme,* cit., pp. 22 e 69.
212 *Il libro delle gemme,* cit., pp. 22.
213 Dal termine ebraico *qan'ana,* 'zelota', 'patriota', in E. Galavotti, L. Esposito, *Cristianesimo primitivo. Dalle origini alla svolta costantiniana,* ed. 2011, p. 36.

Twelfth Foundation: Amethyst

The amethyst was kept in high esteem too. Cecco d'Ascoli states that 'it helps the intellect and the drunk man'[214]. Like 'a drop of water mixed with wine'[215], in medieval times its quartz were embedded in the episcopal rings, in order to remember the wine from the *Last Supper*. Hildegard believed it effective against the dull or stained skin. It was believed that if exposed to fire, stone became white to imitate diamond, and that it would take away vipers and snakes[216]. Considered of equal value to the ruby, emerald and sapphire, it was called 'humility stone' because it was believed able to dominate the pride, to donate reason and lead to introspection[217], as well as to reduce the anger and have benefits on stress, leading to a deep and peaceful sleep.

The twelfth amethyst base relates to the apostle Matthias (short for *Mattathias*, 'chosen by God'); In fact, he was chosen by the Holy Spirit to take over Judas Iscariot. The choice came with a draw, through which the divine preference fell on him and not on the other candidate, Joseph called 'Barsabbas'. Matthias was present in the *Cenacolo* at Pentecost; later he began to preach, but there is no further information about him. Perhaps he died in Jerusalem and its relics were brought to Trier from St. Helena, Emperor Constantine's mother.

---

214 Cecco d'Ascoli, *L'acerba,* cit., III, XVII, v. 18.
215 D. Compagni, *L'intelligenza,* cit., p.12.
216 *Il libro delle gemme,* cit., pp. 43-44.
217 *Il libro delle gemme,* cit., p. 44.

7. *Ultima Cena* (1507 ca.) conservata nel Museo Da Vinci (Abbazia di Tongerlo),
Part. degli apostoli a sinistra del Cristo (Tommaso, Giacomo il Maggiore e Filippo).

*Last Supper, preserved at the Da Vinci Museum, Tongerlo. The apostles on the left
of Christ (Thomas, James the Elder and Philip - © 2016 - News-Thill / Sofam - Belgium).*

The use of stones in the Sforza age: fashion, jewelry and biblical tradition

In the Renaissance precious stones were of great importance, because, in addition to their protective function, considered primary and indispensable in the earlier medieval age, jewelry had a further, equally important purpose which was always inseparable from the former: its ornamental function.

For the duration of the fifteenth century, economic progress and increased wealth were the order of the day. This led to an artistic and cultural renaissance which resulted, in the court milieu, in the need to adopt a more refined way of dressing. As Giorgio Marangoni has noted, the Renaissance saw Italian fashion taste at its apex with Italian styles becoming a mark of the highest distinction at European courts. Not only clothing but also accessories emerged from Italian cities which produced gems and cameos of international fame[218]. Lombardy and Tuscany were the largest export centres in Italy with Milan beginning to excel in the production and restoration of precious stones and Florence, thanks to a renewed interest in classicism, becoming a centre for gems and antique cameos collection[219]. In the Renaissance, the production of valuable jewellery was no longer the goldsmiths' exclusive competence; many artists were also jewellery artisans, and they joined corporations that guaranteed them protection and privileges. Artists such as Donatello and Botticelli, only to name a few, had begun their activities entering as apprentices in a goldsmith's workshop.

In the fifteenth century, the renewed interest in classicism favoured the further spread of gems and the revival of the Roman style, which in imperial times planned to apply them to closure of fur and coats through a precious buckle, generally consisting in garnets. In the Renaissance, pearls, precious gems and stones were set in central pendants, necklaces and brooches to be applied on clothes. Especially pins and large brooches were pinned on belts, corsets and capes to emphasize richness and refinement of taste.   The precious ornament research involved both women and male fashions, accessories such as hats, gloves, fur and even boots had to have an applied jewel, as evidenced by the extensive Renaissance portraiture[220].

---

218 G. Marangoni, *Evoluzione storica e artistica della moda – dalle antiche civiltà al Rinascimento*, Milano 1985, pp. 225-227.

219 F. Tasso, item 'Glittica', in *Arti minori*, dictionary edited by C. Piglione, F. Tasso, Milano 2000, p. 158.

220 G. Marangoni, *Evoluzione storica della moda*, cit., pp. 225-227.

In the Lombard field, jewellery had flourished for centuries, and it had produced great works already in the Lombard period, as the Sforza age now claimed an almost millennial tradition. Specifically, courtly fashion wanted a large use of precious stones, both natural and artificial. Although the canonical sources, as Vasari and Lomazzo, do not speak of a direct contact of Leonardo with the precious arts, we know that Leonardo was familiar with stones. He had, in fact, trained with Andrea Verrocchio who also worked as a goldsmith at his workshop in Florence[221]. Many artists were engaged and thus Lorenzo the Magnificent summoned the best goldsmith restorers from Milan. On the other hand, there was nothing difficult about sourcing precious stones in the Duchy of Milan. Morigia has argued that, in the Milan area, stones as carnelian, jacinth, rubies and amethyst were certainly available[222]. However, as Paola Venturelli has noted, the demand for gems likely exceeded availability to the point that counterfeiting was necessary and in Milan this led to the birth of a flourishing craft trade.

At the Sforza court Leonardo himself had applied himself to the formulation of recipes for making synthetic gems[223]. It is not known for certain whether he practiced the goldsmithery and hard stone carving arts which he was certainly familiar with. But we do know that he designed also jewelry, perhaps stimulated by the opportunities offered by court life including weddings, anniversaries and events. As Mazenta recalls, 'in Arts' workshops, many machines that were discovered by Leonardo were used to cut, slick crystals, irons, stones'[224]. Leonardo da Vinci first in Florence, and later in Milan, had breathed this cultural climate. Echoing a widespread fashion in the Sforza court and entering the signet-stone in the Last Supper, the teacher showed attention toward the Lombard goldsmith tradition, which in the liturgical furnishings, ornamentation and fashion, involved a wide use of gems, and not only for aesthetic purposes. Set in a wedding ring, rather than in a pendant or a necklace, precious stones were placed as a sign capable of referring to specific meanings.

In *Fermagli*, anthology of short stories by Fabricio Luna published in 1536 following the *Vocabulario di cinquemila vocabuli toschi non men oscuri che utili e necessarj del Furioso, Bocaccio, Petrarcha e Dante [...]*, the author cites symbols and allegorical inscriptions engraved on the jewellery to transmit encrypted messages,

221 M. Barasch, *Luce e colore nella teoria artistica del Rinascimento*, Genova 1992, p. 66 (tit. or. *Light and color in the Italian Renaissance, theory of art*, New York University, 1978).

222 P. Morigia, *Historia dell'antichità di Milano*, Milano 1592, p. 268; Paola Venturelli, *Gioielli e gioiellieri milanesi, Storia, arte, moda (1450-1630)*, Milano 1996, p. 52.

223 P. Venturelli, *Leonardo da Vinci e le arti preziose*, Venezia 2002, p.105 s.

224 G. A. Mazenta, *Alcune memorie dei fatti di Leonardo da Vinci a Milano e dei suoi libri*, Milano 1991, pp. 30-31, 40.

as amorous phrases, values and virtues[225]. In courtesan society, they were pinned on the precious robes, cloaks and headdresses to convey messages to interpret. In this regard, what we read in *Dialogo dell'imprese militari e amorose,* published posthumously in 1555 is effective, where Paolo Giovio, speaking of the clips, wrote 'which the great lords and noble knights of our times bring in overcoat, bards and flags to signify part of their generous thoughts'[226]. Open to the size of the game and the fun offered in the Court room, Leonardo too had drawn riddles and allegories for clothing and perhaps destined to a specific client[227].

It is interesting to notice that most of the characters of the *Last Supper*, as in the Roman fashion, are dressed with a coat and tunic with neckline adorned with a stone-bezel. Considering the state of conservation in which the gems painted by Leonardo have come down to us, it is very difficult to go back to their eventual enigmatic function, although at the Sforza court, clasp stones were also used for this purpose. However, we know that the Sforza's Milanese treasure that had gone lost with the arrival of the French in Milan in 1499, was very rich: Ludovico il Moro was aware that the gems, universal symbol of authority and power, conveying the concept of wealth, gave back the identity to the wearer. Clasps with pearls diamonds and rubies were sophisticated and rich gifts of symbolism; in 1480, the Duke himself had donated to his sister-in law Bona of Savoy a clasp bearing the initials 'GB' (Galeazzo, his son, and Bona)[228].

In addition to the ornamental function, in the Renaissance minerals continued to preserve their evocative power and they continued to be associated with a specific value. Ficino suggested for example against the plague to hold in the mouth and neck a ruby, 'the virtue of which is so much against poisons'[229], and again in the eighth decade of the sixteenth century, Giovanni Paolo Lomazzo found that use of gems in fashion 'must consider their virtues meanings'[230], and provided information regarding the colour and tone of stones, the requirements on which their own power depended[231]. Lomazzo recalls for example that the beryl benefit the intellectual faculties, the sapphire made the man pure and diamond

225 F. Luna, *Vocabulario di cinquemila vocabuli toschi non men oscuri che utili e necessarj del Furioso, Bocaccio, Petrarcha e Dante nuovamente dichiarati e raccolti da Fabricio Luna per alfabeta ad utilità di chi legge, scrive e favella,* G. Sultzbach, Napoli 1536, p. 113 s.
226 P. Giovio, *Dialogo delle imprese militari e amorose,* Lione 1559, p. 6;
227 P. Venturelli, *Leonardo e le arti preziose,* cit., p. 15.
228 ASMi, Sforzesco, cart. 1483, 1459, aprile 7.
229 M. M. Ficino, *Il consiglio di M. Marsilio Ficino Fiorentino contro la pestilentia, con altre cose aggiunte appropriate alla medesima malattia,* Venezia 1556, p. 72.
230 G. P. Lomazzo, *Trattato dell'arte della pittura, scoltura e architettura,* Milano 1584, p. 133.
231 G. P. Lomazzo, *Trattato dell'arte,* cit., Libro VI, cap. LIX, pp. 466-68.

favoured loyalty and love[232]. Ruby instead symbolized the blood and Christ's charity, and as it was believed to benefit human vitality[233], it was embedded in wedding rings as a wish for many children[234]. The astral meaning too had been handed down, so that Paolo Lomazzo stated:

The same sky is crowned with twelve stones, according to the elements, which ancient Aaron had in the rational almost four rows of precious stones in the form of planets[235].

Thanks to the ancient and medieval texts, the symbolism of the stones had then stored: on the other hand, in the fifteenth century the *Lapidaries* were still considered, and as recalled by Paola Venturelli, thanks to a translation published in 1476, Leonardo knew the *Naturalis Historia* by Plinio and medieval texts, such as the *Secreta* by Albertus Magnus and the *Acerba* e *Fiore di Virtù*[236] by Cecco d'Ascoli, all works present in his personal library, as well as perhaps a Lapidary referred to the text of St. Albert the Great or Marbod[237]. Although he used to define himself as 'man without academic study', the artist also attends public libraries, where he had access to scientific manuscripts[238].

It is therefore logical to think that the focus and rigor that the artist devoted to the painting design, from the prospective plant to the distribution of the figures on the table, to the vegetation that adorns the bottom of the tapestries, were also adopted in order to study the details considered 'minor', if not completely neglected by posterity, as the stones-bezel, which at the time had not gone unnoticed. As Pietro Marani says, the *Last Supper* is a work that needs to be examined considering 'on the one hand the culture omni comprehensive and eclectic of the big genius da Vinci, while on the other the client and the religious

232 G. P. Lomazzo, *Trattato dell'arte,* cit., Libro VI, cap. LIX, p. 133; Marbodo, *De Lapidibus preciosij,* Vienna 1511, tit. 3, tit. 18, tit. 26.
233 P. Castelli in *L'oreficeria nella Firenze del Quattrocento,* edited by in M. C. Ciardi Duprè, Firenze 1977, pp. 343-345.
234 L. Dolce, *Libri tre nei quali si tratta delle diverse sorti delle gemme che produce la natura,* Venezia 1565, c. 29r, cc. 35R-v.
235 G.P. Lomazzo, *Trattato dell'arte della pittura,* cit., Libro VI, cap. LIX, p. 466. Also S. Epifanio was considered, see A. Bacci, *Delle XII pietre pretiose, le quali per ordine di Dio nella santa legge adornavano la veste sacra del Sommo Sacerdote,* Roma 1587.
236 *Fiore di Virtù* is in the list of books, read (and perhaps owned) by Leonardo, and is present as f. 210ar of the *Codice Atlantico.*
237 P. Venturelli, *Leonardo e le pietre preziose,* cit, p. 78. In-depth analysis see G. D'Adda, *Leonardo da Vinci e la sua Biblioteca,* Milano 1873.
238 M. Barasch, *Luce e colore nella teoria artistica,* cit., p. 69.

environment in which the artist found himself working ', and to whom the painting was intended[239], a Dominican convent of the Observance, whose order had been rooted in Milan since the early years of its foundation[240].

In the time in which Leonardo's activity was carried out, Vincenzo Bandello was prior of the monastery of Milan (1495-1501), and he was awarded in 1484 the title of 'Magister in theology', the highest award of the Dominican Order[241]. Since the art project had to satisfy both Moro and the prior, before Leonardo set his hand to the brush, the iconographic program was carefully examined not only from the patron, lord of the richest Italian court at that time, but also by the Dominican friars, preachers who were especially dedicated to the study and evangelization. Meeting the different stakeholders had to be far from simple for Leonardo: the artistic technique used required long execution times and the prior, tired of the discomfort caused by the scaffoldings that had rendered unusable the refectory to the community for three years, urged often the teacher to continue the work to faster rhythms[242]

Figuration itself had generated discordant opinions among the friars: the triad on the right of Christ appeared squeezed up and their heads were too close; Leonardo had then painted Peter with the knife in his hand, ready to hit the high priest's servant in the 'Garden of Olives', while his left hand was going to fit under John's chin. The discontent among the friars had to be general, and the climate of exasperation had often caused discussions between the brothers. Moreover, the work, depicting the farewell dinner of the Master with the small community of disciples with remarkable realism, went to adorn the environment where religious consumed meals, and by virtue of the *Last Supper* of Christ with his, the Dominican spirituality considered the refectory a sacred place: as Vincenzo Bandello reminds in the *Declarationes super diversos passos Constitutionum* of 1505, before entering it was necessary to follow a ritual that involved, among other things, washing their hands and praying before the Holy Cross.

239 P. C. Marani, *Il Cenacolo di Leonardo,* Milano 1986, p. 11 s., e P. Brambilla Barcilon, P.C. Marani, *Leonardo. L'Ultima Cena,* Milano 1999.

240 Gruppo artistico 'Taccuino democratico', *Monasteri e conventi in Lombardia: ricerca e documentazione dalle origini al 1500,* Milano 1983, p. 50 s.

241 Per V. Bandello, in relazione al rinnovamento di Santa Maria delle Grazie. See: M. Rossi, Novità per Santa Maria delle Grazie (pp. 15-34), in 'Arte lombarda', 66, 1983.

242 G. Vasari, *Le vite de' più eccellenti pittori, scultori e architettori*, Firenze 1568, III, p. 6; G. B. Giraldi, *Discorsi intorno al comporre de i Romanzi, delle Comedie e delle Tragedie, e di altre maniere di Poesie*, Venezia 1554, p..201.

In the refectory, people received the blessing and listened to a passage of the Scripture; then one could start the meal, always respecting the total silence[243]. According to the observant Dominican spirituality, the environment of the cafeteria had also to offer to the monks the opportunity to turn their thoughts to the mystery of salvation, focusing their gaze on the contemplation of future realities.

Leonardo had not yet received an adequate religious formation and it is logical to wonder where he drew the iconography of precious stones on; however, as Macaluso reported, the teacher claimed that 'the religious speculation should be left to the brothers, fathers of populations, who by inspiration know all the secrets'[244]. We do not know to what extent the suggestions received, the biblical commentaries consulted, the sermons or conversations with the brothers in the Dominican convent, had approached Leonardo to the Gospel teachings. Certainly, in the Milanese monastery the teacher could easily access to the Scriptures and biblical commentaries. Since the Dominicans dedicated themselves to evangelization and to the study, it was probably the same religious people, and especially the prior Bandello, prominent theologian, who indicated biblical references to the artist as well as the precious details, although still leaving him a wide room for interpretation[245]. On the other hand, Leonardo could not stand the religious impositions, to the point of choosing not to paint the halos to the characters in the *Cenacolo*[246]. However, the insertion of stone-jewels satisfied certainly both the patron and the recipients of the work. Although we do not know if the Duke's private collection was an inspiration for the artist and whether he has drawn from there the details of the stones-bezel for the symbolism of the *Last Supper* of Santa Maria delle Grazie, certainly Moro could see the gems that he estimated both worn by Christ and by the apostles. In turn, the religious people, knowing the biblical symbolism related to minerals, were lowered more deeply into the mystery of the Jesus's Last Supper thanks to the painting: at an eschatological level, the precious stones sent back to not only the figure of the high

243 Text edited in V. Bandello, *Regula Sancti Augustini et Constitutiones Fratrum O. P. emendatae*, 3., *Declarationes super diversos passos Constitutionum Ordinis Fratrum Praedicatorum recolectae ex actis capitulorum generalium per sacre theologie professorem fratrem Vincentium de Castronovo prefati ordinis Magistrum generalem*, Mediolani 1505, c. 36v; ibidem, 2., *Librum Constitutionum Fratrum Ordinis Praedicatorum que per Reverendissimus patrem Magistrum Vincentium de Castro Novo magistrum ordinis fuere correcte*, cc. 3r-3v.

244 G. Macaluso, *Maestri di saggezza. Prima dispensazione*, Roma 1974, p. 126.

245 As noted by Rossi, the *Last Supper* within the monastery would express the Dominican contribution to the work, *Dopo Leonardo. Nuovi contributi lombardi all'iconografia dell'Ultima Cena*, in *Il Cenacolo di Leonardo*, cit., p. 118.

246 D. A. Brown, *Stile e attribuzione*, in J. Shell, D. A. Brown, P. Brambilla Barcilon, *Giampietrino e una copia cinquecentesca dell'Ultima Cena*, Milano 1988, p. 23.

priest and the temple, but also to the blessedness of the heavenly city, ancipated by the reality of the monastery[247].

In particular, Vincenzo Bandello had shown interest in the 'theology of bliss' in a pamphlet written around 1470[248]; later on, when at the insistence of the Moro he had created the ducal chapel on the apse of the Graces, he had resumed the pattern of the heavenly Jerusalem[249], described in Revelation as cube-shaped, like the Holy of Holies in the Temple[250]. The *Book of Revelation* spoke of a new liturgical space, the heavenly temple that took the place of the ancient temple of Jerusalem. Similarly, the Dominican architecture appeared based on a square shape with three round windows on each side, and based on the Dominican Saints[251]. As recalled by Ciccuto, by revisiting the 'metaphysics of light' that found total fulfilment in the dome of the grandstand, Bandello had made the ducal mausoleum 'a foretaste of heavenly blessedness'[252]. Therefore, the emotional involvement of the friars had to be intense and profound, especially when considering that in the Cenacolo and not only in relation to the Jewish breastplate, Leonardo had placed the stones on the neckline of the vest at the heart level, new theological place of worship of the Father[253]. The stones worn by the characters in the Cenacolo are therefore set in votive pins that refer to the ownership of Christ and to the new Israel, the Church, founded on the apostles themselves. In this regard, the relationship between hoshen-apostles is more highlighted if you consider that the last meal of Christ with his people took place in the traditional Jewish rite. Although we do not know for certain whether the iconography of the stones in the Cenacle reports to the Book of Exodus, rather than the Revelation, it is to note that the tight construction of Da Vinci's figuration reminds the 'breastplate of the high priest Aaron': by grouping the characters in groups of three with Christ at the centre, the new High Priest, Leonardo restated Trinitarian setting of the rational where the stones are placed in groups of three in four horizontal rows (see diagram on chapter of Sforza

247 M. Rossi, *Disegno Storico dell'arte lombarda,* Milano 2005, p. 79; *Novità iconografiche e compositive del Cenacolo Vinciano,* in *Il Cenacolo di Leonardo. Cultura domenicana, iconografia eucaristica e tradizione lombarda,* Milano 1988, p. 24.

248 P. O. Kristeller, *A Thomist Critique of Marsilio Ficino's Theory of Will and Intellect. Fra Vincenzo Bandello da Castelnuovo O.P. and His Unpublished Treatise Addressed to Lorenzo de' Medici,* in *Harry Austryn Wolfson Jubilee Volume,* English Sect., II Gerusalemme 1965, pp. 463-94; Bandello, *Opusculum de beatitudine,* in P. O. Kristeller, *Le Thomisme et la pensée italienne de la Renaissance,* Conférence Albert-le-Grand 1965, Montréal-Parigi 1967; M. Rossi, *Vincenzo Bandello, Ludovico il Moro e Leonardo,* in *Il Cenacolo di Leonardo,* cit., p. 68

249 Rev 21,16.

250 1King 6,20.

251 M. Rossi, Vincenzo Bandello, in *Il Cenacolo di Leonardo*, cit., p. 68.

252 M. Ciccuto, *Figure d'artista. La nascita delle immagini alle origini della letteratura*, Fiesole 2002, p. 102; M. Rossi, *L'Osservanza domenicana a Milano: Vincenzo Bandello e l'iconografia della beatitudine nella cupola di S. Maria delle Grazie,* "Arte Lombarda", 1986.

253 John 4,24.

age), as well as the distribution of the twelve gates of the holy city, divided into groups of three at the four Cardinal points. This structure can be seen in the characters of the Cenacolo, to which the teacher assured, with some exceptions, a stone-bezel. The apostles-tribes relationship is remarkable if one considers, as it was noted by David Flusser, that the Qumran community at the time of Christ was directed by a board of twelve priests, taken from Isaiah pesher[254] just like the twelve precious stones on the breastplate of Aaron[255].

Belonging then to the sphere of the divine, the Exodus stones reminded concepts that exceeded their real contingency, and as they were the very manifestation of the Invisible, they were thought as a mystic sign by which God revealed himself and his glory. Proof of this is the fact that minerals are placed in the breastplate in 3 vertical rows (3 is the Trinitarian number) distributed on 4 horizontal registers (4 perhaps indicating the Temple of Jerusalem)[256], that is to say 3x4 (12 is the number of the patriarchs), the result of which symbolizes the alliance of Yahweh with his people. If one considers the link between Christ-priest and the twelve apostles, the choice of Leonardo to propose the stones of the rational in the Last Supper takes on the value of a recovered kingship:

> Then Peter said in reply, «See, we have left everything and followed you. What then will we have?» Jesus said to them, «Truly, I say to you, in the new world, when the Son of Man will sit on his glorious throne, you who have followed me will also sit on twelve thrones, judging the twelve tribes of Israel»[257].

The scientific aspect of Leonardo's masterpiece has also to be considered. Indeed, if the purpose that moved Leonardo was knowledge, then this was investing every aspect, even beyond the same artistic doing. His approach to things was very broad: he had done his apprenticeship in the workshop of Verrocchio, a painter, sculptor and goldsmith, as well as a mathematician, geometrician and optics[258].

---

254 Ancient manuscripts comments of Jewish origin; for further study, M. Burrows, *The Dead Sea scrolls of St. Mark's Monastery*, I, *The Isaiah manuscript and the Habakkuk commentary*, New Haven 1950.

255 D. Flusser, *Qumran und die Zwölf*, in *Initiation, studies in the History of Religions*, Leyde 1968, p. 134 s.; D. Flusser *The Pesher of Isaiah and the twelve apostles*, in E. L. Sukenik Memorial Volume, EI 8, 1967,52-62 (hebr.).

256 Israel drew perhaps the symbolism of numbers from the Egyptian culture. Number four was about the symbolism of the Egyptian temple, where only the high priest entered, representing the pharaoh (priest-kings) R. Lachaud, *Magia e iniziazione nell'Egitto dei faraoni. L'universo dei simboli e degli dei, spazio, tempo, magia e medicina*, Roma 1997, p. 150.

257 Mt 19,27-28

258 G. Vasari, *Le vite de' più eccellenti pittori*, cit., III, p. 357 s.

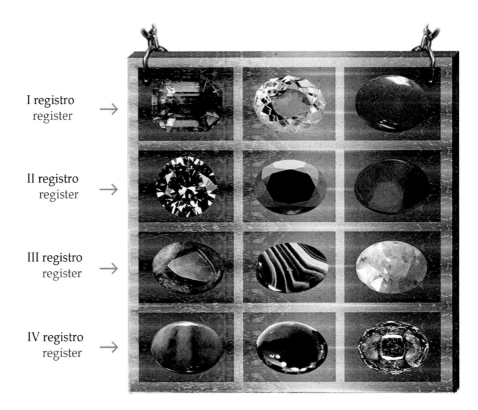

I registro
register →

II registro
register →

III registro
register →

IV registro
register →

Gli aspotoli presentano lo stesso criterio distributivo delle pietre sullo hòshen
In the Last Supper you see the same distribution of the stones on the breastplate

Great observer of reality, the Master from Vinci chased the eternal becoming of light and colour. In addition to the study of optics that he was deepening, in 1491, a few years before starting the *Cenacolo*, he got his hands on *Code C*[259], in which he explored the behaviour of light and shadows, he analysed the effects of different light sources, the light of the stars, and he reported his research on the phenomena of reflection and refraction[260], such as those generated by the light passing through a prism. That is not all. At the Sforza court, Leonardo had become friend with the Franciscan friar Luca Pacioli[261], a mathematician, theologian and philosopher[262]. Since 1494, Pacioli had become interested in the geometry of nature and cosmos, a theme that he had developed in *De Divina Proportione*, concluded in 1498[263], in which he explained the divine presence hidden in the mathematical criterion that gave order to the universe. The meeting with Luca Pacioli corresponded to an intensification of studies of mathematics and geometry by Leonardo[264] who was fascinated by the topic of divine proportion, to such extent that he graphically illustrated the Platonic polyhedral[265] for the Treaty of Pacioli[266]. The regular polyhedral, also called 'cosmic figures', were detectable in nature in crystals and some minerals. The precious stones, cut into various shapes according to the type of mineral, offered the artist not only a chance to play with the effects of light, that was the spiritual element par excellence, a symbol linked to the very concept of bliss, but they also allowed him to illustrate the cosmic harmony much sought after by Vincenzo Bandello and announced in apocalyptic text.

259 The *Code C* (1490), containing 28 pages on light and shadow, it is conserved at the Institute of France (Paris).

260 M. Barasch, *Luce e colore nella teoria artistica del Rinascimento*, Genova 1992, p. 61 s.

261 Pedretti remember that the friendship between the two scientists had as a first result of the book *Divina Proportione*, *Studi vinciani: Documenti, Analisi e Inediti leonardeschi*, Ginevra 1957, p. 44.

262 C. Scarpati, *Leonardo scrittore*, Milano 2001, p. 61.

263 The work was published in Venice in 1509. (treccani.it/enciclopedia/luca-pacioli/ (last visit: 05.09.2016).

264 S. Cremante, *Leonardo da Vinci. Artista, scienziato, inventore*, Firenze 2005, p. 39; N. Sala, G. Cappellato, *Viaggio matematico nell'arte e nell'architettura*, Milano 2003, p. 25.

265 They are the five regular polyhedra: the tetrahedron (triangular pyramid), the hexahedron (cube); the octahedron (formed by eight equilateral triangles); dodecahedron (formed by twelve pentagons); icosahedron (of twenty equilateral triangles). Probably the interest of the Pythagoreans for Platonic solids sprang observing the pyrite crystals present in the Magna Grecia. As mentioned, the *Book of Revelation* describes the holy city cube-shaped (Rev 21,16). See also G. T. Bagni, B. D'Amore, *Leonardo e la matematica*, Milano 2006.

266 L. Pacioli, *De divina Proporlione*, a cura di A. Marinoni, Cinisello B. 2010.

Finally it must be noted that the Master from Vinci devoted himself to the study of physiognomy portraying people in real life and defining the 'human types he employed for the faces of the apostles, each with a specific individual character'[267]. As written by Flavio Caroli, in his drawings the teacher was looking for the 'movement of the soul' and its manifestation on the facial features of the face, to the point of interpreting the painting itself as the mirror of the soul[268]. In one of the preparatory drawings of *the Last Supper*, perhaps related to the figure of Judas Iscariot (W. 12555r), the artist observed:

When you make your figure, think well who he/she is and what you want him/her to do, and make the work look like to the intent and the pretension.

The stones bezel were probably associated with the characters of the *Cenacle* also with regard to this aspect. In this respect, Giorgio Vasari (1511-1574) wrote in his *Le Vite*:

For Leonardo imagined and succeeded in expressing that anxiety which had seized the Apostles in wishing to know who should betray their Master. For which reason in all their faces are seen love, fear, and wrath, or rather, sorrow, at not being able to understand the meaning of Christ; which thing excites no less marvel than the sight, in contrast to it, of obstinacy, hatred, and treachery in Judas; not to mention that every least part of the work points out an incredible diligence[269].

So considering all the foregoing reasoning, especially the artist's multifaceted personality capable of assimilating art and scientific knowledge; the use of gemstones-bezel during the Sforza period and the religious environment in which he found himself working, it is easier to admit that Leonardo not only did not randomly choose the gems, but he also painted with awareness, enriched by the knowledge that he had matured until then. On the other hand, it would be

---

267   David Alan Brown, *Quando l'Ultima Cena era nuova*, in *Il genio e le passioni, Leonardo e il Cenacolo. Precedenti, innovazioni, riflessi di un capolavoro*, by P. C. Marani, Milano 2001, p. 263; Berdini in *Magia e astrologia nel Cenacolo di Leonardo*, Roma 1982, p. 14. He recalls that Leonardo had deepened the Arab physiognomy studies.
268 F. Caroli, *Leonardo. Studi di fisiognomica*, Milano 2015.
269 G. Vasari, *Le vite de' più eccellenti pittori, scultori*, cit., tomo IV, p. 34 s.

difficult to think that a genius of such magnitude who chased the sublime in every detail – to the extent of trying out the paradox of reproducing the same effects of an oil on canvas with a fat tempera on the wall had neglected the stone with bezel, painting them without a good reason. It makes more credible the idea that, as he considered other details and allegories within the composition, in the same way he painted the gems carefully, paying special attention to each of them.

Since the artist, as it has been mentioned knew the classical sources and the medieval *Lapidary*, which were still subject of interest during the Renaissance, the stones-bezel of the *Cenacle*, far from being an object of value for this world, would be 'celestial stones' of great splendour, a symbol of the heavenly Jerusalem and the charisms of each apostle. Therefore, in its uniqueness, Leonardo described the Lord's Supper as an event in which implications on several fronts are traceable and we must learn to read and interpret them.

Leonardo and the stones in the Last Supper painting: interpretation hypotheses

Twenty-year long restoration work (1977-1999) led by Pinin Brambilla Barcilon made visible, and sometimes recognisable, some of the twelve stones mentioned in the *Books of Exodus* and *Revelation* painted by Leonardo in his *Last Supper*. Reading the work from left to right, the gems that appear in the work correspond to James the Less, Andrew, John, Christ, James the Greater, Philip, Matthew and Simon the Zealot. Unfortunately, because of the inexorable deterioration which the painting has been subjected to, not all the stones have been preserved in such a way as to allow for immediate identification. One possible interpretation can still be tentatively made on the basis of a comparison between Leonardo's masterpiece and numerous existing copies. The *Last Supper* has been copied over the centuries, initially by Leonardo's pupils, and later by artists with their easels standing in the refectory of the Dominican monastery making 'live' copies of a work whose image was initially simply due to their copies[270]. There are hundreds of reproductions of Leonardo's *Last Supper* worldwide painted on a range of mediums such as Flemish tapestry woven in Brussels between 1505 and 1515, the canvas copy by Cesare Magni, 1520, at the Pinacoteca di Brera, the *Last Supper* on panel painted by Van Dyck in 1618 and by Vespino[271] and the copy, also on wood, by Giovan Battista Bianchi dated 1790.

---

270 For in-depth about the copies, see N. Bertoglio Pisani, *Il Cenacolo di Leonardo da Vinci e le sue copie*, Pistoia 1907; L. Horst, *L'Ultima Cena di Leonardo nel riflesso delle copie e delle imitazioni*, "Raccolta Vinciana", XIV, 1930-34, pp. 118-200.

271 G. Bossi remember that was commissioned by Federico Borromeo, and only later acquired by the Biblioteca Ambrosiana, *Del Cenacolo di Leonardo Libri Quattro*, Milano 1810, p. 271.

The earliest works, made in the Leonardo milieu in the early decades of the sixteenth century, made as realistic copies of the original, are generally the most reliable and constitute credible evidence of many, once lost but now again visible, details. Among the many copies, this study has taken into account those considered most reliable. In chronological order:

- **1507.** *The Last Supper* (perhaps by) Andrea Solario kept at Tongerlo (Belgium).

- **1508.** *The Last Supper* housed in the refectory of the Monastery of San Sigismondo in Cremona attributed to Tommaso Aleni.

- **1515 ap.** The Marco da Oggiono *Last Supper* in the Museum of the Renaissance at Ecouen.

- **1515 ap.** *The Last Supper* by Giampietrino, owned by the Royal Academy of Arts in London.

- **1537 ap**. The copy preserved in the Episcopal Seminary of Savona, work perhaps of Giampietrino.

- **1547-67.** *The Last Supper* by Cesare da Sesto, preserved in Ponte Capriasca in Ticino.

However it has not been yet considered the lost copy of Castellazzo attributed to Solario[272], certainly among the most faithful ones, but of which unfortunately there are only black and white pictures, and therefore not useful to the recognition of the minerals. The *Supper* of Tongerlo (fig. 8) is attributed by Möller to Andrea Solario[273] (Milan, 1465 - 1524), probably a pupil of Leonardo who painted it around 1507. In 1545, it was purchased by abbot Streyters for the Abbey of Tongerlo, and was the pride of the former abbey church in the last centuries. Damaged in 1929 because of a fire, it was restored by Arthur Van Poeck, and so preserved since 1966 in the Museum da Vinci of the Abbey of Tongerlo.

---

272 L. Steinberg, *Leonardo's Last Supper*, 'The Art Quarterly', 1973, App. C, pp. 409-10.
273 R. H. Marijnissen, *Het da Vinci-Doek van de Abdij van Tongerlo*, Tongerlo 1959; L. Steinberg, *Leonardo's Last Supper*, 'The Art Quarterly', XXXVI/4, 1973, p. 404.

8. *Ultima Cena* attribuita ad Andrea Solario (Museo Da Vinci, Tongerlo).
The Last Supper *of Tongerlo, probably painted by Andrea Solario*
(Da Vinci Museum, Tongerlo - © 2016, News -Thill / Sofam - Belgium).

9. *Ultima Cena* conservata nel Monastero di San Sigismondo a Cremona.
The Last Supper *preserved in the Monastery of San Sigismondo, Cremona, Italy*
(for kind courtesy of the Ufficio Beni Culturali, Diocesi of Cremona).

Contemporary to with the previous one is the *Last Supper* of Tommaso Aleni from Cremona, said 'the Fadino'[274], a painter active between the late fifteenth and early sixteenth century who painted a fresco of it around 1508. The painting adorns the refectory of the Dominican convent of San Sigismondo in Cremona (fig. 9, 66)[275]. The painting (fig. 13, 57, 58) attributed to Marco da Oggiono[276], follower of Leonardo, is attributable to the second decade of the sixteenth century and has smaller dimensions (cm. 260 x 549) than the original (cm. 460 x 880). Owned by the Louvre, it is now preserved at the Musée de la Renaissance in Écouen Castle. It has many details related to the copy of Tongerlo.

The *Last Supper* (fig. 10, 11, 60) on canvas dated around 1515, it is attributed to Giampietrino, artist documented from 1508 to 1549, and it has slightly lower dimensions (cm. 302 x 785) than the original Da Vinci[277]. The painting, owned by the Royal Academy in London, is currently on display at Magdalen College, Oxford. We do not know nothing of its origin, who commissioned the painting, or its original position. We only know that it was preserved in the Certosa di Pavia (1626), but it is unlikely that this was his initial position. According to Malvezzi, it was probably commissioned by one of the sons of Ludovico il Moro, Massimiliano and Francesco, and only later it was donated to the Certosa of Pavia[278]. In 1821, it was acquired by the Royal Academy in Londonas the work of Marco da Oggiono. Although it was cut at the top, this copy in oil on canvas is an important reference for the reconstruction of some lost details of the original painted from Da Vinci.

More difficult is the attribution of the canvas, less known, of the Episcopal Seminary in Savona (fig. 12, 56, 67). Maybe it is comparable to the presence of Marco from Oggiono in Liguria, and Battista da Vaprio probably produced it in the early sixteenth century[279]; or instead, it may be the work of Giovan Pietro Rizzoli, said 'Giampietrino', who painted it in 1537, when he was called to Savona from a local confraternity[280].

---

274 treccani.it/enciclopedia/aleni-tommaso-detto-il-fadino_ (Dizionario-Biografico)/ (last visit 27.08.2016).

275 L. Steinberg, *Leonardo's Last Supper*, cit., XXXVI/4.

276 Marco da Oggiono was a Lombard artist (approx. 1475-1530); C. Marcora, *Marco d'Oggiono*, Oggiono-Lecco 1976, pp. 66-67; C. Bertelli, *Leonardo e l'Ultima Cena* (ca. 1495-97), in AA.VV., *Tecnica e stile di pittura murale del Rinascimento italiano*, a cura di E. Borsook e F. Superbi Gioffredi, Firenze 1986, p. 36.

277 According to P. Marani the artwork is instead attributed to Giovanni Antonio Boltraffio (1467-1516).

278 L. Malvezzi, *Le glorie dell'arte lombarda*, Milano 1882, p. 187.

279 C. Varaldo, *Un'opera leonardesca nella Liguria di ponente. Il polittico di Marco d'Oggiono e Battista da Vaprio per il S. John di Andora*, 'Rivista ingauna e intemelia', 1976-78, XXXI-XXXIII, pp. 164-71.

280 B. Barbero, *La quadreria del Seminario di Savona*, by C. Doglio, Savona 2006, p. 56.

10. Giampietrino, *Ultima Cena.*
   The Last Supper *by Giampietrino* (©Royal Academy of Arts, London)

11. Sotto: gli apostoli a sinistra del Cristo. *Below: the Apostles on the left of Christ*

12. L'*Ultima Cena* conservata nel Seminario vescovile di Savona. Forse venne dipinta da Giampietrino nel 1537, durante un suo soggiorno a Savona. (Per gentile concessione del Seminario Vescovile di Savona).

The Last Supper preserved at the Episcopal Seminary of Savona. The work was probably painted by Giampietrino in 1537, during his stay in Savona. (For kind courtesy of the Episcopal Seminary of Savona).

13. Sotto: gli apostoli a sinistra di Cristo. *Below: The Apostles on the left of Jesus. photo © RMN-Grand Palais (Musée de la Renaissance, château d'Ecouen) / Gérard Blot.*

The copy kept in the parish church of Saint Ambrose in Ponte Capriasca, in the Canton Ticino (fig. 14, 15, 55) dates from a few decades later. Made with frescoes with tempera finish, the work adorns the left transept of the building, and it was probably created by Cesare da Sesto, another student of Leonardo who carried it out by 1567[281]. Despite the awkward manner of some figures and some details less cared for, the well-preserved work bears the names of the individual apostles at the bottom, this suggests that it may have been performed when Leonardo's original figures were no longer distinguishable. It is smaller than the original (cm. 361×559), and it is less reliable than the previous copies; therefore, we will consider only those details of this work in agreement with the other copies.

The works by Leonardo's pupils offer the possibility of a valuable comparison in order to rebuild what the *Cenacle* has been irretrievably lost. In particular, the copies by Giampietrino (fig. 8, 60) and Tongerlo (fig. 10, 11), very similar between them, have proved to be fundamental for this research. The Flemish tapestry woven in Brussels between 1505 and 1515, now in the Vatican Museums, and the micro mosaic composed between 1810 and 1817 by the Roman artist Giacomo Raffaelli (1753-1836) for Napoleon Bonaparte, and now preserved in the Minoriten Kirche in Wien, must be added to the sixteenth-century copies. Even if it traces back to the early nineteenth century, the work still presents some interesting details; however, only those details in accordance with the copies already mentioned and considered most faithful to the original Da Vinci have been taken into consideration as regards as this *Supper*.

As mentioned in the previous chapter, the medieval *Lapidaries* continued to be important until the Renaissance, and we know that Leonardo was familiar with the ancient texts, to the extent that through the associations wanted by the artist, ancestral components are traceable and Leonardo probably translated them in choices that are not only cultural, but also emotional. Depending on the symbolic value and virtues of gems, the Master painted the minerals according to the charisma, personality and inner life of each character. However, in the *Last Supper*, the artist followed a distribution criterion that would seem to reveal a greater autonomy in exposing his mystical of the stones. Then we examine the stones inherited from the biblical tradition and the medieval one that with the exception of the Iscariota, associated a stone to each apostle (see diagram in the chapter of Stone's symbology). We will start examining the most easily identifiable stones, trying to explain their interpretation by da Vinci; we will then rebuild those that are no longer legible.

---

281 The work is witnessed in the pastoral visit that year, Milano, Archivio della Curia, *Visite pastorali delle tre Valli svizzere*, vol. 23, f. 172.

14. Cesare da Sesto, *Ultima Cena*, Chiesa di Sant'Ambrogio,
    Ponte Capriasca (Cantone Ticino).
    Cesare da Sesto, Last Supper, *Church of Sant'Ambrogio,*
    Ponte Capriasca (Cantone Ticino, Switzerland).

15. Gli apostoli Giacomo il Minore ed Andrea.
    The apostles James the Less and Andrew.

Finally, we will talk about the stones that Leonardo preferred to hide or not paint at all, trying to identify the reasons for his choices. In the *Cenacolo,* the stones that appear intact and complete are those related to the apostles Andrew and John. Andrew, Peter's elder brother, is located in the *Last Supper* as the third figure on the left (see diagram after fig. 15). The paint film of its stone is well preserved (fig. 16-17) and shows a very nice mineral, oval and blue sky coloured, set in a thick little visible gold on the ochre robe and on the edge of the neckline. The reflections of the stone would seem to point to a turquoise or a light sapphire, with a smooth and bright surface.

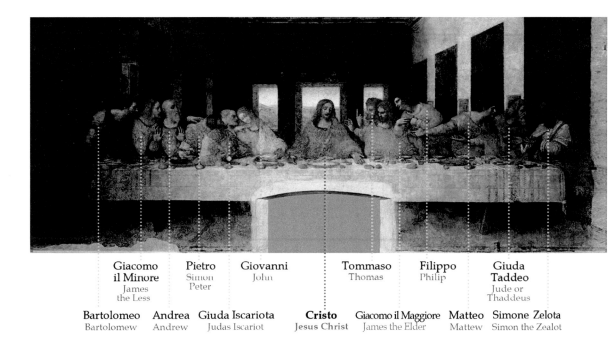

Giacomo il Minore James the Less	Pietro Simon Peter	Giovanni John	Tommaso Thomas	Filippo Philip	Giuda Taddeo Jude or Thaddeus

Bartolomeo Andrea Giuda Iscariota **Cristo** Giacomo il Maggiore Matteo Simone Zelota
Bartolomew Andrew Judas Iscariot **Jesus Christ** James the Elder Mattew Simon the Zealot

Schema della distribuzione dei personaggi nel *Cenacolo* di Leonardo
Scheme of the distribution of the characters in the Leonardo's Last Supper

The copy of Tongerlo (fig. 18) and the mosaic of Giacomo Raffaelli show a clear and nice stone, blue-grey colour. As we mentioned, the medieval tradition attributed to Andrew the II foundation of the heavenly city of sapphire stone, considered among the most valuable.

As regard as this association, in the late sixteenth century the discalced Carmelite Emanuele di Gesù Maria wrote:

> *To the appearance of Andrew the most subtle deceptions and finest fraud of the clever snake remained uncovered... the best sapphires are the ones that discover the blue of the native colour and some ruby vein, with the blood that turned limbs of the churchyard into ruby his body because of the fury of lashes... and even Andrew seems to me that he had those souls in the hands, who wanted to put them in corpses. Andrew proved to be not only greedy of the cross, but also in love as if it were his bride. In addition, this love was so fervent that brought him out of himself, as usually happens in all of lovers' souls[282].*

We do not know for sure if the one painted on Andrew's garment is a sapphire; however, we know the medieval tradition, related the apostle to this mineral. In addition, the stone painted on John's garment is clearly visible (fig. 19-20) and allows to identify with certainty a silver-grey stone, a wonderful *Yahalom*, mounted on a silver bezel. Queen of all gems, this diamond in the Renaissance was still considered a symbol of luxury and wealth, as it is documented by the wide portraiture[283].

The *Suppers* examined, in which the detail is readable, bear the same gem with the characteristic effects of transparency, assembled on a silver base (copies by Tongerlo fig. 22, and Raffaelli fig. 24) or gold (copy by Giampietrino, Royal Academy of Arts, London, fig. 23, 63). In the *Supper* from Cremona (fig. 21), the stone has no bezel.

---

282 Fra' Emanuele di Gesù Maria, *Fiori del Carmelo sparsi nelle festività de' santi. Panegirici sagri,* Napoli 1680, pp. 562 e 569.
283 P. Vezzosi, *È lui il più bello: ritratti medicei nella villa-museo di Cerreto Guidi,* Firenze 2007, pp. 14-15

16.

17.

Part. della pietra-castone dipinta da
Leonardo sulla veste di Andrea (16 e 17);
la stessa pietra nella *Cena* di Tongerlo (18).

The stone in the Leonardo's Last Supper
(16-17) and in the copy of Tongerlo (18,
(©2016 - News-Thill / Sofam - Belgium).

18.

Unlike other gems, which all have oval shape, John's stone presents the right circular cut of the diamond, but without facets: moreover, the gem was only polished at the surface at least until Renaissance, to the extent that in 1599 Friar Emanuele di Gesù e Maria wrote:

It is more than a century that diamonds began to be polished that way; what put them in greater reputation and esteem is working on the ornament, and therefore anyone who wants to appear will always prefer the one that will attract the most the gaze of others[284].

By relating the diamond to John, if on the one hand Leonardo was distancing himself from a tradition that linked the young apostle to the emerald, on the other he showed attention to the virginity of the beloved disciple of the Lord. Edmondo Solmi reminds us for example that Leonardo in his studies also reported the *Acerba* and *Flower of Virtue* by Cecco d'Ascoli, who believed that wearing a diamond meant to be invincible as it scared away spirits and irreducible enemies[285]. Mineral characterized by high brightness and hardness, the diamond associated with John was effective not only in terms of shiny spirituality of the apostle, but also because the 'the disciple whom Jesus loved'[286] was the only one having spread its faith in the resurrection of the Master, and he remained calm not only with the announcement of betrayal during the Dinner, but also under the cross[287]. However, the emerald painted on the robe of Christ is intriguing: the unusual relationship deserves a thorough discussion, which is taken up later. The other stones, whose painting film is visible only in part or it is entirely gone, are not of easy detection. However, the emerald painted on the robe of Christ is intriguing: the unusual relationship deserves a thorough discussion, which is taken up later. The other stones, whose painting film is visible only in part or it is entirely gone, are not of easy detection. The confrontation with the students' copies, however, allowed to envisage the original gems. Leonardo also associated a stone with James of Alpheus (see diagram after fig. 15), depicted in profile, and with great resemblance to Christ, of which he was a cousin on his father's side. The painting film related to its gem is only partially visible (fig. 25-26).

284 Fra' Emanuele di Gesù Maria, *Fiori del Carmelo,* it., p. 752 s.
285 M. J. Kemp, *Lezioni dell'occhio: Leonardo da Vinci discepolo dell'esperienza,* Milano 2004, p. 57; E. Solmi, *Vita segreta di un genio,* Roma 2013; *Il libro delle gemme,* cit., p. 59.
286 John 13, 23; John 19,26; John 20,2; John 21,7; John 21,20.
287 John 19,26.

Part. del diamante dipinto da Leonardo sulla veste di Giovanni (19 - 20); la pietra nelle copie di Cremona (21), Tongerlo (22), Giampietrino (23) e Raffaelli (24).

The diamond painted by Leonardo on the dress of Andrew (19-20); the stone in the copies of Cremona (21), Tongerlo (22), Giampietrino (23, Royal Academy of Arts, London) and Giacomo Raffaelli (24).

However, the fragments of pigment are sufficient to indicate a bluish stone, assembled on a gold signet of oval shape. We know that the Middle Ages associated James the Minor with topaz, which in addition to the 'Imperial' variety with solar tones, the blue hue is also known, more or less intense. The copies by Tongerlo (fig. 28) and Giampietrino (Royal Academy of Arts, London, fig. 27 and 29) depicted a blue-grey stone, while the gem does not appear in the *Last Supper* by Marco da Oggiono (fig. 58) and in the *Supper* from the Episcopal Seminary of Savona (fig. 59). As we have said, the tradition associated the topaz with this apostle.

The pigment of James Zebedee's stone fell completely (fig. 31), as there are only a few fragments of colour of the gold setup. While the Fadino bears an ornament composed of more gems, in the *Suppers* of Giampietrino (fig. 34), by Cesare da Sesto (fig. 32), from Savona, Tongerlo (fig. 30, 33), in the copy of Marco da Oggiono (fig. 61) and in the mosaic of Raffaelli the gem appears reddish-brown, which is the typical shade of carbuncle, a stone associated in the Middle ages to this apostle, and highly widespread during the Sforza age[288].

The carbuncle associated to James the Greater's recognized the strong character and 'fire' virtues of the apostle[289], depicted in the *Last Supper* while it shows a strong reaction to the announcement of the imminent betrayal. James the Great was a man of great faith and ardent charity[290] and 'carbuncle', easily confused with ruby in ancient time, was translated into Greek *anthrax*, meaning 'glowing coal'[291], which considered the stone capable of giving force[292]. On the other hand, James was the first apostle who suffered martyrdom[293].

Continuing our reading, we meet the beautiful figure of Philip: Leonardo paints the apostle standing with his hands over his heart while he rises candidly and wonders whether he betrayed the Lord[294]. Its gem is really deteriorated (fig. 36). The few anthracite grey pigment residues are barely sufficient to identify an oval mineral assembled on a gold bezel.

---

288 It was found in the area of Bellinzona, P. Venturelli, *Gioielli e gioiellieri milanesi, Storia, arte, moda (1450-1630)*, Milano 1996, p.52.

289 The Gospel calls the sons of Zebedee, James and John, *boànerges*, which means 'sons of thunder' (Mk 3,17; Lk 9,52-56).

290 Santiebeati.it (last visit: 20.08.2016).

291 M. G. La Grua, *Cristo nelle pietre preziose*, cit., p. 34.

292 *Il libro delle gemme*, cit., pp. 42-43.

293 E. Milano, P. Di Pietro Lombardi, M. Ricci, A. M. Venturi Barbolini, Biblioteca Estense(Modena), Legenda aurea. Iconografia religiosa nelle miniature estensi, Modena 2001, p. 20.

294 Mt 6,22.

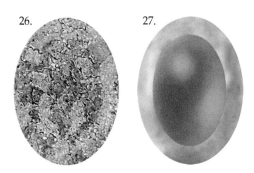

Part. della pietra-castone sulla veste di Giacomo il Minore (25-26); la stessa pietra nella *Cena* di Tongerlo (28) e nella copia di Giampietrino (27 e 29, Royal Academy of Arts, London)

The stone painted by Leonardo on the dress of James the Less (25-26); the same stone in the paintings of Tongerlo (28) and Giampietrino (27-29) (Royal Academy of Arts, London)

In the copies, however, the stone is visible: the copy of Savona, Giampietrino (fig. 37, Royal Academy of Arts, London), Solario (fig. 35, 38), Marco da Oggiono (fig. 61) report a dark gem, with grey-brown or grey-green hues, which is the natural colour of agate and green sardonyx. We need to recall that the Middle Ages associated Philip with the sardonyx, variety of onyx with darker bands of colour, thought to be capable, among other things, to keep humble and chaste anyone who wore it[295]. The stone refers to the concept of pure heart. The painting film on the robe of the young figure of Matthew has totally fallen. Only the yellowish base stretched by the Master as a primer preparation has remained (fig. 40). Giampietrino (fig. 42), the artist of Tongerlo (fig. 39, 41) and Marco da Oggiono (fig. 62), however, reported a grey-purple coloured gem, perhaps identifiable with amethyst which was associated by one part of the tradition with Matthew[296]; the copy of Savona reports instead of a stone with olive-green hues: we need to remember that the medieval tradition attributed to Matthew a stone from the greenish colour of varying intensity, the chrysolite, linked to the concept of penance in relation to Matthew who had been called by Jesus to change his life[297].

The final character of the *Last Supper* at which Leonardo associated a stone is Simon the Zealot, represented on the right at the end of the table, while he is consulting with Thaddeus. The tiny pigment fragments make the eighth gem unrecognizable despite the fact that the golden oval set can be glimpsed (fig. 44). Again, the comparison with the copies by the students has proved essential to go back to the possible original stone painted by the master.

The *Supper* by Giampietrino (fig. 45) and those of Savona, Tongerlo and Marco da Oggiono (fig. 62) show a reddish-orange stone, that remembers a jacinth. As we have said, the jacinth, whose colour varies from orange of various levels of brightness to brown, from the medieval tradition was attributed to Simon the Zealot. Jacinth was used in exorcisms and was believed to protect travellers in foreign lands[298]. It was associated with a range of virtues depending on colour[299].

---

295 *Il libro delle gemme*, cit., p. 27.
296 S. Cavenago-Bignami, *Gemmologia*, cit., p. 862.
297 Lk 5,27-28.
298 *Il libro delle gemme*, cit., pp. 22-23 e 69.
299 S. Cavenago-Bignami, *Gemmologia*, cit., p. 644.

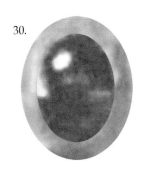

30.

31.

32.

La pietra sulla veste di Giacomo Maggiore, non più visibile nel *Cenacolo* (31), appare di colore bruno rossiccio nelle *Cene* di Tongerlo (30, 33), di Cesare da Sesto (32) e di Giampietrino (34).

The stone of James the Elder is not still visible in the Cenacolo (31); It is brown-reddish in the copies of Tongerlo (30, 33), of Marco da Oggiono (32) - photo © RMN-Grand Palais (musée de la Renaissance, château d'Ecouen)/Gérard Blot), and Giampietrino (34 - Royal Academy of Arts, London).

33.

34.

Leonardo does not therefore link all his characters with a stone but chose not to paint some of them and conceal others, such as that relating to Simon Peter, pictured with John at the Saviour's right hand (see diagram after fig. 15). Man by the reactive character, surprised by the revealing words of Christ, he snaps forward to know the traitor's name (fig. 63). His impulsiveness will take him a few hours later to draw the sword that will hit the high priest's servant, in an attempt to prevent the capture of the Master, who will heal Malchus remembering the apostle that 'those who take the sword will die by the sword'[300]. Leonardo depicted indeed Peter with the knife in his hand, ready to strike, while the figure of Judas, drawing back to the proclamation of Christ, is hiding the stone that adorns the robe of the apostle (see diagram after fig. 15). If it is true that the Lord entrusted to Peter the keys of the Kingdom of Heaven[301], in the *Supper* of Santa Maria delle Grazie the primacy of the apostle is shortly overwhelmed by his human nature: in the course of that night, the disciple would betray his Master by saying he 'does know the man'[302]. Leonardo illustrated the distance of Peter's heart from the law of love through the refusal of showing his bezel-stone, which leaves us only guessing, although the medieval tradition has associated the green jasper with the apostle, symbol of fortitude in faith as illustrated[303]. Not surprisingly, the mineral is defined as:

> *True hieroglyphics of the Apostle St. Peter, the rudest and lowest of all in Nature but the most sublime and unparalleled among the gifts of grace so the Jasper is the first of the fundamentals, because among all the Apostolic Stones, only Peter befits the Primacy. First in the eminence of merit, first in the Faith stead-fastness and first in the likeness that he contracted with Christ[304].*

---

300 Mt 26,51-52.
301 Mt 16,13-28.
302 Mt 26,74.
303 S. Cavenago-Bignami, *Gemmologia*, cit., p. 863.
304 Fra' Emanuele di Gesù Maria, *Fiori del Carmelo*, cit., p. 517.

35.

36.

La pietra relativa a Filippo nella
Cena Vinciana (36) è poco leggibile.
Nella copia di Tongerlo (35-38)
presenta colore grigio-bruno;
è di tonalità grigio-verde nella
copia di Giampietrino (37).
(Royal Academy of Arts, London).

37.

*The stone painted on the mantle
of Philip in the Last Supper (36)
is no longer readable. In the copy
of Tongerlo (35-38) it has a gray-brown
indefinite color; in the copy of
Giampietrino it is gray-green (37)
(Royal Academy of Arts, London).*

38.

Similarly, Leonardo hides the stone relative to S. Thomas (fig. 54), the doubting apostle who will ask the Lord to put his hand into his side to be able to believe in the resurrection. Appearing to his disciples after his resurrection, the Lord invited the disciple to see for himself the reality of his resurrection:

> Now Thomas, one of the Twelve, called the Twin, was not with them when Jesus came. So the other disciples told him, «We have seen the Lord. But he said to them, «Unless I see in his hands the mark of the nails, and place my finger into the mark of the nails, and place my hand into his side, I will never believe.» Eight days later, his disciples were inside again, and Thomas was with them. Although the doors were locked, Jesus came and stood among them and said, «Peace be with you.» Then he said to Thomas, «Put your finger here, and see my hands; and put out your hand, and place it in my side. Do not disbelieve, but believe.» Thomas answered him, «My Lord and my God!»[305].

Only after recognizing him Lord and God, Thomas was able to get into Christ's chest, 'rewarding the staggering of faith with constancy of soul and hardness of heart with an ardent charity'[306]. Just like aquamarine, the virtues of mercy and charity were associated with the beryl by virtue of its clarity related to St. Thomas[307]. As mentioned, the stone-bezel that Leonardo painted on the garment of Christ deserves special attention (fig. 48). Despite the extensive falls of the paint film (fig. 47), the restoration of the work of art has made it possible to distinguish a green gem of oval cut, identifiable with an emerald, mineral whose use had widespread in Europe, especially after the discovery of the Americas[308]. It was possible to distinguish the 'oriental' emerald, also called 'the old rock Emerald'[309], characterized by a lighter green and coming from Cyprus and from various European countries; and the 'Western' emerald[310], imported from Central America and characterised by a more intense and high-quality green. The author of the *Supper* of Tongerlo (fig. 50) Giampietrino (fig. 64) and Marco da Oggiono   (fig. 65) place on a dark green stone on the neckline of the Savior, while Raffaelli inserts a stone of an intense brilliant green in his Viennese mosaic (fig. 46), the same gem that we find in the Vatican tapestry (fig. 51) weaved between 1505 and 1510.

---

305 John 20,24-28.
306 Emanuele di Gesù Maria, *Fiori del Carmelo,* cit., p. 778.
307 S. Cavenago-Bignami, *Gemmologia,* cit., p. 659.
308 C. Piglione, F. Tasso, item 'glittica', in *Arti minori,* cit, p. 153.
309 M. De La Harpe, *Compendio della storia generale de' viaggi,* Venezia 1782, vol. 10, p. 151; *Atti dell'Accademia italiana di scienze, lettere, ed arti,* Livorno 1810, Vol. 1, parte 1, p. 46.
310 E. Chambers, *Dizionario universale delle arti e scienze,* Genova 1775, p. 161.

39.

40.

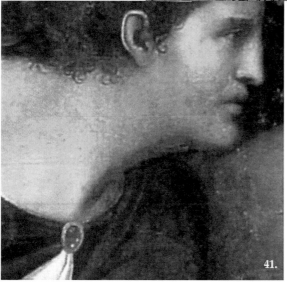

41.

La pietra dipinta da Leonardo
sulla veste di Matteo non è più
visibile, resta solo la base di fondo
stesa dall'artista (40). Nella *Cena*
di Tongerlo (39 e 41) presenta
il color violetto dell'ametista;
nella copia di Giampietrino (42)
il colore è un grigio-viola scuro.
(Royal Academy of Arts, London).

*The stone on the dress of Matthew
in the Leonardo's painting (40)
is no longer visible. In the copy of
Tongerlo (39-41) the stone looks
like an amethyst, and in the copy
of Giampietrino has a indefinite
color dark gray-violet (42, Royal
Academy of Arts, London).*

42.

Attributing the emerald to Christ, Leonardo dissociates himself not only from the Jewish tradition, which assigned the precious ruby (actually a carbuncle) to the tribe of Judah[311], but he also distanced himself from the folk tradition that, relatively to the order of vocation of the apostle and to *Revelation* 21, associated the emerald to St. John. The artist from Vinci then opted for a major shift. Undoubtedly, a green coloured stone on the fire-red robe of Christ would have gained more prominence, than the ruby mentioned in the biblical version of the Vulgate, and we know that in order to highlight the colour combinations, Leonardo kept in his paintings in addition to the colour realism criterion[312] even that of complementarity, considering that the pairs of colours which are opposite to each other, such as red-green and blue-yellow-orange, stand out in a particular way and exalted each other[313]. However, if this were the only criterion used by the master, no one would understand why it had not been adopted for the stones in the apostles' robes. We can assume that in order to paint the stones in the *Last Supper*, Leonardo had not referred to the description in *Exodus* 28, but to the *Revelation* 21, a text that had probably been indicated as a reference by the prior. In any case, Vincenzo Bandello, Master of theology of the first order and leader of a Dominican community of Observance, had thoroughly investigated the Scriptures and in particular John's text, so he would never have accepted a symbolism different from the biblical one if not properly motivated.

We know that the artist knew the value of symbols, to which he was much attracted and frequently employed in his paintings as concrete expressions of the content he wanted to depict. To understand his conceptually valid choice, we must assess the significance that the stones had in antiquity. We know that from ancient civilizations onwards precious stones have been accorded great importance. They have been considered good omens and peacemakers, symbols of spring, responsible for awakening positive moods, the chance for regeneration and the force for good encompassed by the earth[314].

---

311 According to the Bible CEI, the tribe of Judah corresponded turquoise. It is noted that the two gems relating to the tribe of Judah, anthrax and turquoise, are the colors that Leonardo attributed to the *Last Supper* to the robes of Christ: red for the tunic, and blue for the cloak.

312 Leonardo da Vinci, *Trattato della pittura,* Catania 1990, p. 190.

313 M. Barasch, *Luce e colore nella teoria artistica,* cit., p. 93-94; *Leonardo da Vinci, The Literaty Works,* a cura di J. P. Richter, 2 voll., London 1939, p. 280.

314 S. Cavenago-Bignami, *Gemmologia,* cit., p. 658-59; R. Lachaud, *Magia e iniziazione nell'Egitto dei faraoni. L'universo dei simboli e degli dei, spazio, tempo, magia e medicina,* trad. di Livia Pietrantoni, Roma 1997, p. 55.

La gemma di Simone lo Zelota non è più visibile (44). Nelle copie di Giampietrino (45, Royal Academy of Arts, London) e Tongerlo (©2016, News-Thill / Sofam - Belgium), presenta colore bruno-rossiccio.

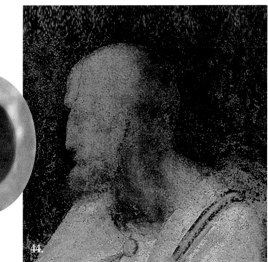

In the Leonardo's Last Supper the stone on the mantle of Simon the Zealot is no longer visible (44). In the copy of Giampietrino (45, Royal Academy of Arts, London), as in the Supper of Tongerlo (43), the stone has a brown-reddish color.

43.

44.

45.

On the heart of the Egyptians mummies they kept a green beetle, symbol of rebirth, while in the Bible the color indicated the vitality of the fair[315]. How remember Luzzatto and Pompas, in the ancient civilizations 'green by simple symbol of the vegetation cover, became a symbol of prosperity, continuity and resurrection, so that the trees from consecrated plants to agricultural deities, were transformed into the same manifestations of their theophany'[316].

Later on, in the Middle Ages, Hildegard of Bingen believed that the emerald was linked to the spring renewal, to the possibility of regeneration and to the good forces contained in the earth[317]. Related to the awakening of nature, the emerald promoted the state of meditation and injected light to the spirit. Hildegard quoted a formula in her *Lapidary* to be recited after overcoming a serious epileptic seizure thanks to the use of the stone:

As the Spirit of God has given life to the world, so corroborate with his grace my body so that it will not falter[318].

Related to the eve of his Christ's Passion, the aforementioned prayer by Hildegard refers to the following passage from Isaiah:

The Lord God is my help; this is why I am not confounded, why I have set my face like rock, knowing I will not be disappointed. Who makes me justice is nearby; who will contend with me? Let us face each other. Who accuses me? Come close to me. Behold the Lord God is my helper: who shall condemn me?[319]

As mentioned, the relic known as *Sacro Catino*, the 'Holy Basin', had always been considered made of emerald, and if on the one hand, the authenticity or falseness of the object does not matter for the purpose of this study, on the other hand it is interesting to note the existence of a tradition that believed that the vessel used by the Lord in the farewell dinner was made of emerald, in relation to the mineral in the garment of Christ.

---

315 Ps 52,10.
316 L. Luzzatto, R. Pompas, *Il significato dei colori nelle civiltà antiche,* Milano 1988, p. 161.
317 *Il libro delle gemme,* cit., p. 20; S. Cavenago-Bignami, cit., p. 658.
318 *Il libro delle gemme,* cit., p. 21.
319 Is 50,7-9 (ESVUK).

46. **47.**

48.

49.

50.

Lo smeraldo dipinto da Leonardo (47-48)
sulla veste del Cristo. La pietra nelle
copie di Giampietrino (49, Royal Academy
of Arts), di Tongerlo (50,©News-Thill/Sofam -
Belgium), nell'arazzo vaticano (51, ricostruzione
grafica) e nel mosaico di Giacomo Raffaelli (46).

*The emerald painted by Leonardo on the dress
of Christ (47-48). The stone painted by Giampietrino (49, Royal Academy of Arts, London),
in the copy of Tongerlo (50, © News-Thill / Sofam -
Belgium), in the Vatican tapestry (51), and in the
mosaic of Raffaelli (46, graphic reconstruction).*

51.

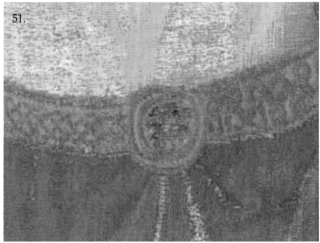

Considering also that the *Last Supper* is a time theologically connected with the Passion[320] as well as the priestly dignity of Jesus by Leonardo[321], the artist's choice could not be accidental: the green colour[322] of the mineral referred to lifeblood of trees, to the Risen Christ and to the inexhaustible life he brought. After greeting the Twelve at the Last Supper, during which he instituted the sacrament of his Body and offered his Blood[323], and after the agony of the Cross in which he entrusted himself in the hands of the Father[324], Christ rose again at Easter, leading all creation and his friends to new awakening, the ones that he found asleep in the Garden of Olives that night, after the meal, three times[325]. Solemn in his lordship, sweet in its abandonment, the Christ-Emerald proposed by Leonardo in the *Supper delle Grazie* showed to the brothers the way of hope that he had travelled himself, in the certainty that the Father would have not abandoned his life in the grave, but he would have filled him with endless joy in his presence[326]. Since that night, in memory of the Bridegroom, the Church celebrated the Lord's Supper, who agreed to share his last meal with those who would have then betrayed him (Judas), denied him (Peter), or would not believe him risen (Thomas), and with all those who would have abandoned him later. However, the names of the twelve apostles are now written on the twelve stones of the heavenly city that indicated the twelve tribes, the pillars of the 'new Israel', the Church[327]: the ancient covenant finds fulfillment in the sacrifice that God makes with his blood. Christ, the new high priest (and the priesthood was prerogative of the Levites, to whom the *hòshen* associated the emerald), is the perfect acceptable sacrifice to the Father for the universal salvation:

When I saw him, I fell at his feet as dead. But he touched me with his right hand, and said, «Fear not! I am the First and the Last and the Living. I was dead, I am alive for evermore, and I have power over death and Hades»[328].

---

320 M. Rossi, *Novità iconografiche e compositive del Cenacolo,* cit., p. 15.

321 M. Rossi, cit., p. 22. For the interpretation of Christ the priest and altar victim, see: J. Snow-Smith, *The Salvator Mundi of Leonardo,* Seattle 1982, and F. Di Giovambattista, *Il Giorno dell'espiazione nella Lettera agli Ebrei,* Roma 2000, p. 119s.

322 P. Vulliaud, ne *Il pensiero esoterico di Leonardo,* trad. di B. Pavarotti, Parigi 1981, Roma 1987, p. 41, he recalls that the Renaissance had its own symbolism of colors.

323 For the sacrifice of Christ and the reality of the Eucharist, E. Cattaneo, *Un milanese a Messa alla fine del Quattrocento,* Milano 1962.

324 Lk 23,46.

325 Mt 26,36-46.

326 Ps 15,8-11.

327 J. Danielou, *La chiesa degli apostoli,* trad. a cura di P. Lunghi, Roma 1991, p. 31 s.

328 Rev 1,17-18 (ESVUK).

Leonardo then associated the emerald to Christ with great effectiveness as a symbol of immortality and hope because the Lord 'makes all things new'[329]. Similarly, the stones worn by the apostles, to whom Jesus transmitted the priestly dignity[330], mean a regained Eden and a recovered royalty, as well as the invitation to participate in his ministry for the universal salvation[331], by virtue of a priesthood which is above the heart and that engage every believer in the way to lost Paradise. Saint Paul, writing to the Church in Corinth, recalled the presence of God in Israel's history and especially during the exodus to the Promised Land: 'They drank of that spiritual Rock that followed them, and that rock was Christ'[332].

By virtue of this membership, St. Paul wrote addressing the church of Ephesus:

> *Consequently, you are no longer foreigners and strangers, but fellow citizens with God's people and also members of his household, built on the foundation of the apostles and prophets, with Christ Jesus himself as the chief cornerstone. In him the whole building is joined together and rises to become a holy temple in the Lord. And in him you too are being built together to become a dwelling in which God lives by his Spirit*[333].

52. The high priest wears the breastplate on the chest
Il sommo sacerdote ebraico indossava lo hòshen sul petto

---

329 Rev 21,5 (ESVUK).
330 M. Rossi, *Novità iconografiche e compositive del Cenacolo Vinciano*, cit., p. 22.
331 Mt 26,26.29.
332 I Cor 10,4 (ESVUK).
333 Eph 2,19-22 (ESVUK).

53. Leonardo's *Last Supper,* the apostles on the right of Jesus - *Gli apostoli a destra di Cristo.*

54. Below, the apostles on the left - *Gli apostoli a sinistra di Cristo.*

Fifty days after Easter, in the Upper Room took place the outpouring who baptized the disciples, making them participants to the royal office of Christ through the seven gifts of the Holy Spirit, ordered for the building of the Church[334]. Similarly, as the twelve foundations of the Heavenly Jerusalem symbolize the Church foundation born at Pentecost, Christian symbology relates a gemstone at each charism given by the Holy Spirit. Of the twelve minerals embedded on the *Hòshen* and of the heavenly city-stone base, the tradition preserved the most precious: sapphire (wisdom), emerald (intellect), amethyst (advice), diamond (fortress), topaz (science), ruby (mercy), chalcedony (fear of God)[335]. The text of *Revelation* 21 then contemplates the state of perfection of the heavenly Jerusalem, filled with the divine Spirit and become the temple itself as a splendid reflection of the glory of God that lives in it together with men. Jerusalem is the city to which the living Lamb communicates life for through the Spirit. In the city of God, all filled gold and precious stones, there is the eternal life as the communion with God is perfect and perpetual and everything has finally reached completion. Leonardo's choice of not to paint all twelve stones deserves a separate speech, as it can be seen by comparing the original *Supper* with copies. To Judas, whose betrayal was separated from the community of the disciples, Leonardo did not associate stone. Judas Iscariot appears wearing a yellow-orange robe, colour that identified people of bad faith and traitor in European art since the Middle Ages[336].

Isolated from the rest by the triad, Christ is represented in the scene without any emotional involvement, already clutching the bag with thirty pieces of silver in his left hand. In the fourth Gospel, we read that when once Judas had dipped the morsel in the common dish with Jesus, he was then invited by the Master to do immediately what he had to do, 'he went immediately out: and it was night'[337].

Curiously, though, Leonardo does not relate the stone-bezel to the apostles Bartholomew and Judas Thaddeus, too. The young Bartholomew depicted on the left side of the table, to whom the medieval tradition attributed the carnelian (see p. 43), appears while pointing hands on the table as those who want to understand what is happening. There were no traces of the setting or the mineral on his robe; the green mantle covers almost entirely the chest, suggesting the edge of the neckline (fig. 58). Similarly, the stone does not appear on the Thaddeus's garment (fig. 45), illustrated on the right while he is consulting with Simon the Zealot.

---

334 The seven gifts of the Spirit are the gifts of which, according to Is 11,2, it was filled the Messiah.
335 A. M. Tripputi, *PGR, Per grazia ricevuta,* cit., p. 108.
336 In the Basilica of Assisi, Giotto had painted cloak of Judas in yellow, while he was kissing Christ in the Garden of Olives.
337 John 13,27-30.

55. The *Last Supper* by Cesare da Sesto (Church of S. Ambrose, Ponte Capriasca)
   Ultima Cena di Cesare da Sesto (Chiesa di Sant'Ambrogio a Ponte Capriasca)

56. The *Last Supper* preserved at the Episcopal Seminary of Savona (Italy)
   Ultima Cena conservata nel Seminario Vescovile di Savona

Similarly, the copies examined do not represent any jewel on the robes of these two apostles.

Bartholomew was an exemplary disciple. He had preached the Gospel in India, and as a result of his testimony, he suffered a terrible martyrdom, being skinned from whipping[338]. Judas Thaddeus, cousin of Christ as his brother James the Minor, was remembered as a generous-spirited man and with an exquisite sensitivity, which earned him the nickname of 'Thaddeus', from Syriac *thad*, 'lovable', 'merciful'. After the descent of the Holy Spirit at Pentecost, he devoted himself first to the evangelization of Judea; then, with Simon the Zealot, he spread the Gospel in Mesopotamia and Persia, operating miracles wherever, casting out demons and getting numerous conversions, including the most legendary that is that of Abgar, king of Edessa. Thaddeus probably died a martyr in Babylon, where he was burned alive[339].

We do not know why Leonardo chose not to associate the gem to these two apostles with an exemplary life. However, we can make some hypothesis. An interesting consideration may be made evaluating the sacredness of the Dominican refectory specifically designed to the receiving of the painting. The work depicted the Lord's Supper, as a preview of the heavenly banquet:

He said to them, «This is my blood of the covenant, which is poured out for many. I assure you that I won't drink wine again until that day when I drink it in a new way in God's kingdom»[340].

After the dinner, the Lord would consume the banquet clad of his glory with his Church and the figuration by Vinci could not but consistently bring the thought of the brothers to the appointment with the Risen Christ[341]. By virtue of the represented scene, no other environment lent itself as the refectory did to welcome the painting.

---

338 santiebeati.it/dettaglio/21400 (last visit: 21.08.2016).

339 santiebeati.it/dettaglio/21900 (last visit: 21.08.2016); sangiudataddeo.net/home.asp (last visit: 21.08.2016).

340 Mk 14,24-25 (ESVUK).

341 The point of view to observe the *Cenacolo* is situated a few meters above, A. Artioli, *Il Cenacolo di Leonardo, Storia, significati, restauri*, in *Il Cenacolo. Il restauro*, Soprintendenza per i beni architettonici e per il paesaggio di Milano, Milano 2002, p. 53.

57. Marco da Oggiono, *Last Supper* (Musée National de la Renaissance, Ecouen)
Marco da Oggiono, *Ultima Cena* (Museo Nazionale del Rinascimento, Ecouen)
(photo © RMN-Grand Palais (musée de la Renaissance, château d'Ecouen) / Gérard Blot.

58. Marco da Oggiono, *Last Supper*. A group of apostles on the right of Jesus.
Marco da Oggiono, *Ultima Cena*. Gruppo di apostoli a destra del Cristo.
(photo © RMN-Grand Palais (musée de la Renaissance, château d'Ecouen) / Gérard Blot.

As mentioned according to the Dominican observant spirituality that was centred on the ultimate meaning of things[342], also the environment where the monks had meals, had to offer them the opportunity to turn their thoughts to the heavenly bliss. This was true to the extent that only after a precise ritual that involved having received the blessing and listened to a passage of Scripture, friars could start their meal, always respecting the silence[343].

The new refectory of the Dominican monastery in Milan had been concluded in 1488[344], and the decision to provide eight windows in the lunettes of the vault was not random. The number eight was considered sacred: St. Ambrose and St. Augustine[345] nurtured a fondness for its symbolism that referred to the sky, to the concept of bliss, eternity and infinity. Moreover, the eight already taken many ancient civilizations refer to a particular symbology.

At the end of the Old Kingdom (2200 BC), the funerary texts of the sarcophagi[346] aimed at ensuring the rebirth of the deceased and the favor of the gods, confirm the importance of the number eight as a symbol of a new beginning and rebirth, as well as cosmic balance. On the *Sarcophagus of Petamon* we read an interesting formula:

I'm the One that becomes Two, I'm the Two that turns into Four, I'm the Four which turns into Eight, and after that I'm the One[347]

In Judaism the eighth day was chosen for circumcision[348], while according to the Kabbalah it indicates the first day of the Creation, the beginning of a new week[349].

---

342 M. Rossi, *Vincenzo Bandello, Ludovico il Moro,* in *Il Cenacolo di Leonardo,* cit., p. 71.

343 Vincenzo Bandello, *Declarationes,* cit., Mediolani 1505.

344 G. Gattico, *Descrizione succinta e vera delle cose spettanti alla Chiesa e Convento di S. Maria delle Grazie e di S. Maria della Rosa,* ms, f. 34; As Marco Rossi remembers in *Il Cenacolo di Leonardo,* cit., p. 70, Domenico Pino wrote that he had read in the lost *Libro dei Consigli,* that in 1481 the monks commissioned the 'fulfillment' of the refectory left 'unfinished' by Gaspare Vimercati, D. Pino, *Storia genuina del Cenacolo insigne dipinto da Leonardo da Vinci nel Refettorio de' Padri Domenicani di Santa Maria delle Grazie di Milano,* Milano 1796.

345 L.F. Pizzolato, *La dottrina esegetica di sant'Ambrogio,* Milano 1978, p. 280-81.

346 It is funerary formulas, bearing magic-religious rituals, mostly written on sarcophagi.

347 *Sarcofago di Petamon*, Museo del Cairo, n. 1160. In-depth analysis, see: J. P. Brach, *Il Simbolismo dei numeri,* by P. L. Zoccatelli, Roma 1999.

348 A. Schimmel, item 'numeri', in *L'uomo e i simboli,* Milano 2002, p. 290.

349 C. Gatto Trocchi, *Enciclopedia illustrata dei simboli,* Roma 2004, p. 263.

59.

The apostles James the Less
and Andrew in the *Supper*
preserved in the Episcopal
Seminary of Savona (59).
Above: the apostles in the
copy of Giampietrino (60).
Royal Academy of Arts, London).

*Gli apostoli Giacomo il Minore
e Andrea nella Cena conservata
nel Seminario di Savona (59).
Sotto: gli apostoli nella copia di
Giampietrino (60, Royal Academy
of Arts, London).*

60.

The eighth day, Sunday, was the day of Christ and his victorious resurrection[350]. In Revelation, John wrote that he had been caught in a trance on 'the Lord's Day', the eighth, which is Sunday and in which the coming of Christ is fulfilled in and whose centre is the Eucharist[351]. The number eight, therefore, refers to the concept of eternity[352]. Leonardo had then deliberately painted eight stones[353], one on the tunic of Christ, and the other distributed on the garments of the seven apostles, another highly symbolic number in the Bible that indicates totality and perfection[354]. As mentioned in the previous chapter, Bandello had set the architecture of the Graces' grandstand according to the exegesis of the Franciscan Alexander from Bremen (d. 1271)[355] whom he had studied in depth the Expositio in Apocalipsim[356]. On the other hand, the Saxon Franciscan had been one of the first to interpret the apocalyptic visions in relation to the history of the Church, including the mendicant orders[357] and highlighting the concept that Francis and Dominic, with their followers, were the saints 'destined to reign with Christ in the final phase of the millennium'[358]. Therefore, the interpretation of the Minorite friar concerned directly the fathers of the Milanese monastery, too[359]. Most probably, it was the Commentary on the Apocalypse by Alexander from Bremen that provided father Bandello with an eschatological interpretation of the elements contained in the text by John, in which the number seven comes back time and time again. There are seven spirits before the throne of God, seven candlesticks[360], seven stars that are the symbol of the angels who watch over the seven Churches of Asia as a symbol of Catholic unity.[361] to which St. John wrote addressing to the Church in its entirety:

---

350 D. Marafioti, *Sant'Agostino e la nuova alleanza: l'interpretazione* agostiniana *di Geremia 31,31-34 nell'ambito dell'esegesi patristica*, Napoli 1994, pp. 127s.

351 *Catechismo della Chiesa Cattolica*, II, 2174, 112.

352 In architecture, the octagon was thus considered a sort of mediation between Square (contingency symbol) and the circle (infinity symbol), and from the fourth century, thanks to the bishop of Milan, St. Ambrose, the octagonal baptismal fonts incorporated the concept of 'passage' from the human condition, to divine sonship.

353 Leonardo, on the advice of a prior friar, had mainly related himself to *Revelation* rather than to the *Book of Exodus*. It is interesting to note that the text of das cites twelve stones, five of which belong to the genus of 'Chalcedony'.

354 Also the multiples of 7 in the Bible are a sign of totality, while half or 7 fractions indicate incompleteness.

355 M. Rossi, *Vincenzo Bandello, in Il Cenacolo di Leonardo*, cit., p. 68.

356 The *Book of Revelation* opens with an invitation to the beatitude: 'Blessed is he who reads and those who hear the words of this prophecy' (Rev 1,3 – Modern English Version, MEV).

357 treccani.it/enciclopedia/alessandro-da-brema/(last visit: 23.08.2016).

358 G. Cremascoli, C. Leonardi, *La Bibbia nel Medioevo*, Bologna 1996, p. 289.

359 Alexander Bremensis, *Expositio in Apocalipsim*, XXI, 1-9, A. Wachtel, Weimar 1955, p. 471.

360 Even the Jewish candlestick had seven branches.

361 L. Biraghi, *Sui due santi martiri Milanesi scoperti nell'anno 1845 presso la Basilica dei SS. Apostoli e di S. Nazaro*, Milano 1855, p. 62 s.

John, To the seven churches which are in Asia: Grace to you and peace from Him who is and who was and who is to come and from the seven Spirits who are before His throne, and from Jesus Christ, who is the faithful witness, the firstborn from the dead, and the ruler of the kings of the earth. To Him who loved us and washed us from our sins in His own blood, and has made us kings and priests to His God and Father, to Him be glory and dominion forever and ever. Amen. I, John, both your brother and companion in the tribulation and kingdom and patience of Jesus Christ, was on the isle that is called Patmos on account of the word of God and the testimony of Jesus Christ. I was in the Spirit on the Lord's Day, and I heard behind me a great voice like a trumpet, saying, «I am the Alpha and the Omega, the First and the Last», and «What you see, write in a book, and send it to the seven churches which are in Asia: to Ephesus, Smyrna, Pergamum, Thyatira, Sardis, Philadelphia, and Laodicea. I turned to see the voice that spoke with me. And when I turned, I saw seven golden candlesticks, and in the midst of the seven candlesticks was one like a Son of Man, clothed with a garment down to the feet and with a golden sash wrapped around the chest. The hair on His head was white like wool, as white as snow. His eyes were like a flame of fire. His feet were like fine brass, as if refined in a furnace, and His voice as the sound of many waters. He had in His right hand seven stars, and out of His mouth went a sharp two-edged sword. His appearance was like the sun shining brightly. The mystery of the seven stars which you saw in My right hand, and the seven golden candle-sticks: The seven stars are the angels of the seven churches, and the seven candlesticks which you saw are the seven churches»[362].

---

362 Rev 1,4-6; 9-16; 20 (ESVUK).

The stones painted in the *Supper* by Marco da Oggiono on the dress of James the Elder and of Philip (fig. 61), of Matthew and Simon the Zealot (fig. 62).

Pietre dipinte da Marco da Oggiono sulle vesti di Giacomo il Maggiore e di Filippo (fig. 61), di Matteo e di Simone lo Zelota (fig. 62).
photo © RMN-Grand Palais (musée de la Renaissance, château d'Ecouen)/Gérard Blot.

John wrote in the chapter 1 that he saw 'seven golden candlesticks', among whom the Son of Man appeared with a garment down to the foot[363], the priestly robe, while 'in his right hand he held seven stars'. In this regard, the monk Alexander from Bremen observed:

The stars are the bishops, who must shine for others with the word and example of life. And even if they have sinned, they are also called stars, for what was established. And he keeps them on the right, that is among the best gifts, which are precisely symbolized from his right hand[364].

The sacrament of the seven stars – it is said sacrament, wherever you see one thing and you mean another - that you saw on my right and the seven golden candlesticks: the seven stars are the angels of the seven churches and the seven candlesticks are the seven Churches[365].

Similarly, in the Rev 3, Christ is called 'He that hath the seven Spirits of God, and the seven stars'[366] and is invested with the fullness of the Holy Spirit that gives him authority over the seven churches. In later chapters, the number seven is in the burning lamps before the throne[367] and in the number of seals that close the open scroll[368] by the lamb that owns seven horns and seven eyes[369]; seven are also the angels who stood before God with seven trumpets. It is therefore likely that Bandello suggested the symbolism of the number seven in Revelation to Leonardo. With the wealth of its eschatology, the last Book of the Bible provided a vision of eternity as no other text of Scripture. Jesus, new Adam and Lord of the eighth day, promised to the winners not only to eat from 'the tree of life which is in the midst of the paradise of God'[370] as a symbol of restored communion between God and man, but he also gave them 'the hidden manna', the Eucharist that is the true heavenly food and a white stone on which 'a new name is written and no one

---

363 Rev 1,12-13 (ESVUK).
364 Alexander Bremensis, *Expositio in Apocalipsim*, cit., I, 19-24, p. 18.
365 Alexander Bremensis, *Expositio in Apocalipsim*, cit., I, 5-11, p. 22.
366 Rev 3,1 (REV).
367 Rev 4,5.
368 Rev 5,5.
369 Rev 5,6.
370 Rev 2,7 (ESVUK). The number seven in the *Book of Revelation* means also the symbol elements of impending doom: the thunder (Rev 10,4), the scourges in the hands of angels and bowls full of divine wrath (Rev 15.5-8).

knows it except who receives it[371]. The reference to the Book of Exodus came back strongly, both in the manna that fed Israel in the desert, and in the white stone as a symbol of light and redemption, on which there the names of the twelve tribes were no longer engraved but they had been substituted with the proper name of each saved. The stones painted in the Last Supper could remember to the friars that Christ, the stone on which they had built their humanity, had prepared a gem for each of them, and the bliss of the New Jerusalem was the promise that awaited them[372]. Alexander from Bremen wrote about this passage:

God had given the opencast manna to the Jews, surpassing the doctrine of Balaam's priests. The names of the jewels embedded in a white colour, that is, the names of the ancients of Israel, of the children; but these are the new names. To whom who wins their doctrine, taught openly, to eat the sacrifices of their idols, and from fornication, and the suffering of those who, by contrast, promises a reward. He gives victory as mentioned above, he curbs the greed of the hidden manna offered, that is, the bread of angels, which are not yet seen by people in all things, and eternal glory, of which the Apostle: What is this, that no eye has seen, nor heard the air? It exceeds white immorality, impurity, because God gives the purity from the nature of the white gem[373].

The promise of Christ was certain and long lasting:

He who overcomes will I make a pillar in the temple of My God, and he shall go out no more. I will write on him the name of My God and the name of the city of My God, the New Jerusalem, which comes down out of heaven from My God, and My own new name. He who has an ear, let him hear what the Spirit says to the churches[374].

---

371 Rev 2,17 (ESVUK).
372 Rev 2,2.14.18; Alexander Bremensis, *Expositio in*, cit., I, 2-1014, p. 26.
373 Alexander Bremensis, *Expositio in Apocalipsim*, cit., II, 1-24, p. 32.
374 Rev 3,12-13 (ESVUK).

63. *Last Supper* by Giampietrino: the stone on the dress of Peter is not visible, because it's covered by the figure of Judas.
Ultima Cena *di Giampietrino: la pietra corrispondente all'apostolo Pietro non è visibile, perché coperta dalla figura di Giuda.*
(Royal Academy of Arts, London).

The Apocalypse ended with a big ritual of praise and exaltation of God's glory, a genuine Eucharistic liturgy:

Alleluia! For the Lord God Omnipotent reigns! Let us be glad and rejoice and give Him glory, for the marriage of the Lamb has come, and His wife has made herself ready. It was granted her to be arrayed in fine linen, clean and white[375].

The Spirit and the bride say, «Come.» Let him who hears say, «Come.» Let him who is thirsty come. Let him who desires take the water of life freely. He who testifies to these things says, «Surely I am coming soon.» Amen. Even so, come Lord Jesus![376]

Since the summit of divine revelation was accomplished in the Eucharist, the eight stones painted in the Last Supper dated back to the communion of Christ with his Church, represented by the apostles with seven stones. Similarly, the Dominican community was called upon to participate to the Eucharistic Lamb Supper in view of the never-ending banquet on the eighth day. The emotional and spiritual participation of the friars had to be profound. Moreover, by suggesting the artist to focus on the centrality of the Eucharist as an anticipation of heavenly bliss[377], Bandello reiterated the Eucharistic theology of St. Ambrose. He had endorsed in his speeches On the Sacraments and on the mysteries the real presence of Christ in the consecrated bread, and the one of St. Augustine, who had emphasized the ecclesial significance[378].

---

375 Rev 19,6-8 (ESVUK).
376 Rev 22,17.20 (ESVUK).
377 In-depth analysis on the Dominican spirituality, see: J. Wasserman, *Reflections on the Last Supper of Leonardo da Vinci*, 'Arte Lombarda', 66, 1983.
378 Some students of St. Augustine of Ippona arrived to affirm that the Eucharist is the Church itself. William of Saint-Thierry, PL 184, 403; the expression 'mystical body' of Christ, began to indicate the Church. The Eucharistic discourse was resumed later in the Dominican area by Tommaso d'Aquino and Antonino of Florence.

64. The Christ painted by Giampietrino. *Il Cristo dipinto da Giampietrino*
    (Royal Academy of Arts, London)

65. The Christ painted by Marco da Oggiono. *Il Cristo dipinto da Marco da Oggiono*
    (photo © RMN-Grand Palais (musée de la Renaissance, château d'Ecouen) / Gérard Blot

Lastly, a final assessment of the number of stones that appear in the *Last Supper* concerns the astronomical level. The Renaissance still held in high regard the celestial phenomena, as the same Ludovico il Moro feared them to the point of referring to Ambrose Varese from Rosate, his doctor and astrologer, to schedule meetings and political affairs[379]. As Berdini recalled, at that time mathematics, astronomy and astrology were closely related and equally endowed with esoteric meanings[380]. The theological discourse of the Prior related to the concept of 'bliss' derived perhaps from the *Tractatus de Glorificatione Sensuum in Heaven* by Bartolomeo Lapacci (1402-66)[381], specially transcribed between 1495 and 1496 for the Library of the Milanese monastery[382]. In his work the Dominican had discussed the properties of the five senses experienced by the Blessed in Heaven[383]. One of the three sections of the treatise examined in particular what the Blessed can experience in its 'seven forms', including listening, speaking and singing[384]. Also involving the Heavens' musical harmony with its seven notes, the mystique of the painting led to a sensory excitement that appealed to the depths of the spirit, in view 'of the things that must soon take place'[385]. In addition to this, Marsilio Ficino, referring to the esoteric doctrine of Hermes Trismegistus[386], had supported in his *De Vita* the ability of the human body to capture the subtle substance that acts on the soul and allows the body to absorb vibrations coming from the sidereal depths.

---

379 P. Venturelli, *Gioielli,* cit., p. 133. On January 13, 1490, in honor of Isabella of Aragon, wife of Gian Galeazzo Sforza, Moro organized a grand theatrical performance (the 'Feast of paradise'), the apparatus in which consistent allegorical children dressed as angels and mythological planets rotating around Jupiter, were designed by Leonardo himself. For further information, G. Lopez, *Festa di nozze per Ludovico il Moro,* Milano 1976, p. 38 s. 152 s.

380 F Berdini, *Magia e astrologia nel Cenacolo di Leonardo*, cit., p. 89.

381 Rimbertini entered at a really young age in the Dominican Order and he was in close contact with Antonino of Florence. In his sermons (preserved by code in Florence, BNC, Conv. Soppr. G.I.646) he highlights the distinguishing characteristics of Dominican preaching, emphasizing the universal value of Latin and Roman union (mirabileweb.it / mel / -bartolomeo -lapacci-de-rimbertini -un-legato-del-papa-nell-europa-centrale-tra-antichit%EF%B%BD-classiche-e-antichit%EF%BF%BD-cristiane/433127 (last visit: 24.08.2016).

382 M. Rossi, *Disegno storico dell'arte lombarda,* Milano 2005, p. 72. For Rimbertini, T. Käppeli, *Bartolomeo Rimbertini (1402-1466), vescovo, legato pontificio e scrittore,* Archivium Fratrum Praedicatorum, 9 (1939): 86-127.

383 K. Pietschmann, *Liturgical Polyphony* and political ambition, in *Religion and the Senses* in *Early Modern Europe,* a cura di W. de Boer, C. Göttler, Leiden-Boston 2013, p. 282.

384 B. Rimbertini, *De deliciis sensibilibus paradisi,* Venezia 1498, fol. 33r.

385 Rev 1,1.

386 For Trimegisto, A. J. Festugière, *La révélation d'Hermès Trismègiste, L'astrologie et les sciences occultes,* Paris 1981, pp. 187-216, e S. Gentile, C. Gilly, *Marsilio Ficino e il ritorno di Ermete Trismegisto,* Firenze 2001, pp. 138-140.

66. The copy preserved at the Monastery of St. Sigismondo in Cremona.
   Part. della copia conservata nel Monastero di San Sigismondo a Cremona
   (for kind courtesy of the Ufficio Beni Culturali - Diocesi di Cremona)

67. Apostles on the left (copy preserved at the Episcopal Seminary of Savona)
   Apostoli a sinistra del Cristo nella copia del Seminario Vescovile di Savona
   (for kind courtesy of the Ufficio Beni Culturali - Diocesi di Savona)

For this purpose, Ficino used these precious stones to create talismans that bore engraved figures in relation with the celestial bodies[387], and employed the musical notes to capture the beneficial effects through the planetary flows[388].

Leonardo certainly had great interest in astrology: as Berdini remembers, the list of books in his library that he drafted himself and documented by the Codex Atlanticus (f. 210 r/a) and the Codes of Madrid (ff. 2v 3v), may confirm the influence of astrology in the cultural education of the Master[389]. As regard as the *Supper* of Leonardo da Vinci, if it is not immediately easy to establish an 'astral inheritance' of the apostles around the Christ in relation to the stones, but as the artist painted only eight of the twelve minerals that are related to the signs of the Zodiac, on the other hand we know that Leonardo harbored a strong admiration for Ptolemy, openly mentioned in the 8936 manuscript of Madrid, f. 3 r (1504-5)[390]. Moreover, although the artist had probably come to guess the heliocentric system[391], at that time the Ptolemaic astronomy was still the one held by the official Church. The Ptolemaic system believed the Earth standing at the centre of the universe, and the seven 'planets'[392] revolved around it, in the background of fixed stars.

The planet known back then were: in order of distance, the Moon, Mercury, Venus, Sun, Mars, Jupiter and Saturn. Taking up the happy expression of Berdini, according to which Leonardo makes the *Last Supper* a 'Ptolemaic sky'[393], it can be assumed that the artist painted the stone related to the planet's astronomical system then in force on the clothes of the seven apostles.

The apostles in the *Supper* were arranged with their own stone around Christ at the centre of the scene, as a reference to the Earth around which the seven planets of the Ptolemaic sky were believed to revolve[394]. The seven stars in the right hand of Christ described in *Revelation* symbolized by the gems in the *Last Supper*, made reference in this case to the superior movement (the heavens). By representing the apostles wearing a gemstone associated with a planet in the

387 T. Katinis, *Medicina e filosofia in Marsilio Ficino: il Consilio contro la pestilenza*, Istituto Nazionale di studi sul Rinascimento, Roma 2007, pp. 49-51.

388 S. Gasbarri, *I busti del Pincio: Nel Giardino della Memoria alla ricerca della nostra identità. Italia, caput mundi della cultura e della civiltà*, Roma 2016.

389 F. Berdini, *Magia e astrologia nel Cenacolo di Leonardo*, cit., p. 89.

390 C. Vasoli, *Le filosofie del Rinascimento*, by P. C. Pissavino, Milano 2002, p. 447.

391 C. Pedretti, *Studi vinciani: Documenti, Analisi e Inediti leonardeschi*, Geneve 1957, p. 121.

392 The term refers to any 'wandering star'

393 F. Berdini, *La Gioconda chi è*, Roma 1989, p. 78.

394 William R. Lethaby, *Architettura misticismo e mito*, a cura di G. Bilancioni, Bologna 2003, pp. 124-126.

system, Leonardo represented the universality of salvation, to which even the constellations were participating with a specific influence. In this work of art, which is strongly Christocentric, the Twelve lurked around Christ[395] as the Lord of the cosmos[396], Beginning and End, the new and eternal Priest, since the work of redemption embraced the twelve tribes of Israel, indicating the saints of all times:

> I heard the number of those who were sealed, one hundred and forty-four thousand out of every tribe of the children of Israel: Twelve thousand from the tribe of Judah were sealed, twelve throusand from the tribe of Reuben were sealed, twelve thousand from the tribe of Gad were sealed, twelve thousand from the tribe of Asher were sealed, twelve thousand from the tribe of Naphtali were sealed, twelve thousand from the tribe of Manasseh were sealed, twelve thousand from the tribe of Simeon were sealed, twelve thousand from the tribe of Levi were sealed, twelve thousand from the tribe of Issachar were sealed, twelve thousand from the tribe of Zebulun were sealed, twelve thousand from the tribe of Joseph were sealed, and twelve thousand from the tribe of Benjamin were sealed[397].

Thus the stones painted by Leonardo, that were so different in their therapeutic properties, assured all possible graces to the heavenly Jerusalem, filled of divine glory. Even this key of interpretation, which examines the universal harmony dealt with in the *Revelation*, may explain the Leonardo's choice to paint only eight stones in the *Last Supper*. It still remains unclear according to which criterion, Leonardo chose the apostles to whom the bezel were associated. Probably, the reason is to be found in the compositional appearance of the work. As there are twelve characters in The *Last Supper* and only eight planets, having deprived, in addition to Judas Iscariot, Peter and Thomas, also Bartholomew and Thaddeus of the respective stone, the lack of association would be less evident, given the more lateral position of these two last apostles in the figurative system of the painting.

---

395 According to F. Berdini, every apostle corresponds to a zodiac sign which embodies the characteristics, *Magia e astrologia nel Cenacolo*, cit., p. 13.

396 corsobiblico.it/apocalisse1.pdf (last visit: 23.08.2016). *Revelation* 21 talks about the Son of Man who holds in his right hand the 'seven stars'.

397 Rev 7,4-8 (ESVUK).

68. Apostles on the right of Christ in the *Last Supper* preserved in Cremona.
Apostoli a destra di Cristo nell'Ultima Cena conservata a Cremona.

Epilogue

At this point, I stop and I leave to the reader, if he wishes, to further advance in the detail of the eschatological stones painted by Leonardo in the *Last Supper*.

I hope I have illustrated it advisedly, without claiming to exhaust the subject, but with the simple intention to re-read the masterpiece in the light of the Scriptures and to offer new ideas of investigation.

Certainly, the issue remains open to further studies, which I am sure, will bring out new truths.

Bibliography

GIUSEPPE FLAVIO, *Antichità giudaiche*, XX, 200.

SIDONIO APOLLINARE, *Epistolae*, I, 8, 12, 46.

ISIDORUS, *Sententiae,* I 10, 15: CCL 111, 34 ; cf. PL 83, 556.

EPIFANIO DI SALAMINA, *De XII gemmis quae erant in veste Aaronis liber*, in Patrologia Graeca 42, coll. 294-304.

G. GATTICO, *Descrizione succinta e vera delle cose spettanti alla Chiesa e Convento di S. Maria delle Grazie e di S. Maria della Rosa,* Milano, Archivio di Stato, *Fondo Religione, p.a.,* cart. 1397.

B. RIMBERTINI, *De deliciis sensibilibus paradisi,* Venezia 1498.

V. BANDELLO, *Regula Sancti Augustini et Constitutiones Fratrum O.P. emendatae,* Mediolani 1505, per Joannem de Castelliono.

MARBODO, *De lapidibus preciosij*, Vienna 1511 *(Liber lapidum seu gemmis).*

F. LUNA, *Vocabulario di cinquemila vocabuli toschi non men oscuri che utili e necessarj del Furioso, Bocaccio, Petrarcha e Dante nuovamente dichiarati e raccolti da Fabricio Luna per alfabeta ad utilità di chi legge, scrive e favella,* Napoli, G. Sultzbach, 1536.

G. B. GIRALDI, *Discorsi intorno al comporre de i Romanzi, delle Comedie e delle Tragedie, e di altre maniere di Poesie,* Venezia 1554.

P. GIOVIO, *Dialogo dell'imprese militari e amorose,* Lione 1559.

G. VASARI, *Le vite de' più eccellenti Pittori, Scultori ed Architettori,* Firenze 1560 (2° ed. 1568) (ed. cons. Milanesi, Firenze 1973).

M. MARSILIO FICINO, *Il consiglio di M. Marsilio Ficino Fiorentino contro la pestilentia, con altre cose aggiunte appropriate alla medesima malattia,* Venezia 1556.

L. DOLCE, *Libri tre nei quali si tratta delle diverse sorti delle gemme che produce la natura,* Venezia 1565.

P. MORIGIA, *Historia dell'antichità di Milano,* Milano 1592.

G. P. LOMAZZO, *Trattato dell'arte della pittura, scoltura e architettura,* Milano 1584 (ed. cons. a cura di R.P. Ciardi, Firenze 1973-74).

BACCI, *Delle XII pietre pretiose, le quali per ordine di Dio nella santa legge adornavano la veste sacra del Sommo Sacerdote,* Roma 1587.

FRATE EMANUELE DI GESU' MARIA, *Fiori del Carmelo sparsi nelle festività de' santi. Panegirici sagri*, Napoli 1680.

P. POLO, *Mansiones Festaque Hebraeorum: Literaliter Descripta Moraliter, Mistice*, Barcellona 1725.

E. CHAMBERS, *Dizionario universale delle arti e scienze*, Genova 1775.

M. DE LA HARPE, *Compendio della storia generale de' viaggi*, Venezia 1782.

D. PINO, *Storia genuina del Cenacolo insigne dipinto da Leonardo da Vinci nel Refettorio de' Padri Domenicani di Santa Maria delle Grazie di Milano*, Milano 1796.

G. BOSSI, *Del Cenacolo di Leonardo Libri Quattro*, Milano 1810.

Acts of Italian Academy of Science, literature and arts, Livorno 1810.

A. TEIFASCITE, *Fior di pensieri sulle Pietre Preziose*, trad. di A. Raineri, Firenze 1818.

F. INGHIRAMI, *Storia della Toscana compilata ed in sette epoche distribuita dal cav. Francesco Inghirami*, Fiesole 1841.

L. BIRAGHI, *Sui due santi martiri Milanesi scoperti nell'anno 1845 presso la Basilica dei SS. Apostoli e di S. Nasazo*, Milano 1855.

D. COMPAGNI, *L'intelligenza*, Milano 1863.

G. D'ADDA, *Leonardo da Vinci e la sua Biblioteca*, Milano 1873.

L. MALVEZZI, *Le glorie dell'arte lombarda*, Milano 1882.

G. CERESETO, *Istituzioni bibliche, ossia introduzione generale e speciale a tutti i libri della Santa Scrittura*, Chiavari 1893.

C. PLINIO IL VECCHIO, *Naturalis Historia*, Karl Friedrich Theodor Mayhoff, Lipsiae, Teubner 1906.

N. BERTOGLIO PISANI, *Il Cenacolo di Leonardo da Vinci e le sue copie*, Pistoia 1907.

I. MASERRI-BENCINI, *L'Egitto secondo gli scrittori antichi e moderni*, Firenze 1912.

CECCO D'ASCOLI, *Acerba*, trad. di A. Crespi, Ascoli Piceno 1927.

L. HORST, *L'Ultima Cena di Leonardo nel riflesso delle copie e delle imitazioni*, "Raccolta Vinciana", XIV, 1930-34.

E. ZOLLI, *Israele, studi storico-religiosi*, Udine 1935.

T. KÄPPELI, *Bartolomeo Rimbertini (1402-1466), vescovo, legato pontificio e scrittore*, Archivium Fratrum Praedicatorum, 9 (1939).

LEONARDO DA VINCI, *The Literaty Works*, a cura di J. P. Richter, 2 voll., London 1939.

Iacopo da Varagine e la sua Cronaca di Genova dalle origini al MCCXCVII. Tipografia del Senato, Roma 1941.

M. BURROWS, *The Dead Sea scrolls of St. Mark's Monastery*, I, *The Isaiah manuscript and the Habakkuk commentary*, New Haven 1950.

C. BARONI - S. SAMEK LUDOVICI, *La pittura lombarda del Quattrocento*, Messina-Firenze 1952.

M. BERNARDI, *Leonardo a Milano*, Torino 1952.

ALEXANDER BREMENSIS, *Expositio in Apocalipsim*, series *Monumenta Germaniae historica*, by A. Wachtel, Weimar 1955.

C. GRÜNANGER, in *Storia della letteratura tedesca. Il Medioevo*, Milano, 1955.

C. PEDRETTI, *Studi vinciani: Documenti, Analisi e Inediti leonardeschi*, Ginevra 1957.

R. H. MARIJNISSEN, *Het da Vinci-Doek van de Abdij van Tongerlo*, Tongerlo 1959.

W. DEINERT, *Ritter und Kosmos in Parzival*, Monaco, 1960.

E. CATTANEO, *Un milanese a Messa alla fine del Quattrocento*, Milano 1962.

P. O. KRISTELLER, *A Thomist Critique of Marsilio Ficino's Theory of Will and Intellect. Fra Vincenzo Bandello da Castelnuovo O.P. and His Unpublished Treatise Addressed to Lorenzo de' Medici*, in *Harry Austryn Wolfson Jubilee Volume, English Sect.*, II, Gerusalemme 1965.

V. BANDELLO, *Opusculum de beatitudine*, in P. O. KRISTELLER, *Le Thomisme et la pensée italienne de la Renaissance*, Conférence Albert-le-Grand 1965, Montréal-Parigi 1967.

ALBERTO MAGNO, *De mineralibus*, ed. Borgnet, trad. (inglese) di D. Wyckoff, *Book of Minerals*, Oxford 1967.

D. FLUSSER, *The Pesher of Isaiah and the twelve apostles*, in *E. L. Sukenik Memorial*, Gerusalemme 1967.

D. FLUSSER, *Qumran und die Zwolf, Initiation*, Leyde 1968.

R. GRAVES, R. PATAI, *I Miti ebraici*, tit. or. *Hebrew Miths*, Milano 1969.

H. KRATZ, *Wolframs Parzival. An Attempt at a Total Evaluation*, Berna, 1973.

L. STEINBERG, *Leonardo's Last Supper*, "The Art Quarterly", XXXVI/4, 1973.

G. MACALUSO, *Leonardo filosofo e profeta*, in *Maestri di saggezza. Prima dispensazione*, Pensiero e Azione, Roma 1974.

A. LIPINSKY, *Oro, argento, gemme e smalti: tecnologia delle arti dalle origini alla fine del Medioevo, 3000 a.C. - 1500 d.C.*, Firenze 1975.

G. LOPEZ, a cura di, *Festa di nozze per Ludovico il Moro*, Milano 1976.

C. MARCORA, *Marco d'Oggiono*, Oggiono-Lecco 1976.

C. VARALDO, *Un'opera leonardesca nella Liguria di ponente. Il polittico di Marco d'Oggiono e Battista da Vaprio per il S. John di Andora*, 'Rivista ingauna e intemelia', 1976-78.

M.C. CIARDI DUPRE' DAL POGGETTO, a cura di, *L'oreficeria nella Firenze del Quattrocento*, Firenze 1977.

J. HANI, *Il simbolismo del tempio cristiano*, traduzione a cura di T. Buonacerva, Parigi 1978.

L. F. PIZZOLATO, *La dottrina esegetica di sant'Ambrogio*, Milano 1978.

S. CAVENAGO-BIGNAMI MONETA, *Gemmologia*, tomo I, Milano 1980.

A. J. FESTUGIÈRE, *La révélation d'Hermès Trismègiste*, I, *L'astrologie et les sciences occultes*, Paris 1981.

P. VULLIAUD, *Il pensiero esoterico di Leonardo*, trad. di Barbara Pavarotti, Parigi 1981, Roma 1987.

F. BERDINI, *Magia e astrologia nel Cenacolo di Leonardo*, Roma 1982.

L. H. HEYDENREICH, *Invito a Leonardo: l'Ultima Cena*, Milano 1982.

J. SNOW-SMITH, *The Salvator Mundi of Leonardo*, Seattle 1982.

GRUPPO ARTISTICO 'TACCUINO DEMOCRATICO', *Monasteri e conventi in Lombardia: ricerca e documentazione dalle origini al 1500*, Milano 1983.

J. WASSERMAN, *Reflections on the Last Supper of Leonardo da Vinci*, "Arte Lombarda", 66, 1983.

C. BERTELLI, *Leonardo e l'Ultima Cena* (ca. 1495-97), in AA.VV., *Tecnica e stile di pittura murale del Rinascimento italiano*, a cura di E. Borsook e F. Superbi Gioffredi, Firenze 1986.

G. DE MONTREUIL, *Perceval*, Milano, 1986.

M. ROSSI, *L'Osservanza domenicana a Milano: Vincenzo Bandello e l'iconografia della beatitudine nella cupola di S. Maria delle Grazie,* Arte Lombarda, 1986.

G. MARANGONI, *Evoluzione storica e stilistica della moda – dalle antiche civiltà al Rinascimento,* Milano 1985.

P. C. MARANI, *Il Cenacolo di Leonardo,* Milano 1986.

D. A. BROWN, *Stile e attribuzione,* in J. Shell, D. A. Brown, P. Brambilla Barcilon, *Giampietrino e una copia cinquecentesca dell'Ultima Cena,* Milano 1988.

L. LUZZATO, R. POMPAS, *Il significato dei colori nelle civiltà antiche,* Milano 1988, p. 161.

M. ROSSI, A. ROVETTA, *Il Cenacolo di Leonardo. Cultura domenicana, iconografia eucaristica e tradizione lombarda,* Milano 1988.

F. BERDINI, *La Gioconda chi è,* Roma 1989.

G. S. ABBOLITO (a cura di), VENERABILE BEDA, *Omelie sul Vangelo.* trad. a cura di G. S. Abbolito, Roma 1990.

G. DEVOTO, A. MOLAYEM, *Archeogemmologia: pietre antiche glittica magia e litoterapia,* Roma, 1990.

LEONARDO DA VINCI, *Trattato della pittura,* Catania 1990.

J. DANIELOU, *La chiesa degli apostoli,* trad. a cura di Pietro Lunghi, Roma 1991.

G. A. MAZENTA, *Alcune memorie dei fatti di Leonardo da Vinci a Milano e dei suoi libri,* Milano 1991.

M. BARASCH, *Luce e colore nella teoria artistica del Rinascimento,* Genova 1992 (original title: *Light and color in the Italian Renaissance, theory of art,* New York University, 1978).

D. MARAFIOTI, *Sant'Agostino e la nuova alleanza: l'interpretazione agostiniana di Geremia 31,31-34 nell'ambito dell'esegesi patristica,* Napoli 1994.

J. M. RIVIERE, *Amuleti Talismani e Pantacoli. I principi e la scienza dei Talismani, nelle tradizioni orientali e occidentali,* trad. di Donatella Rossi, Roma 1994.

A. ROMANO, *Federico II legislatore del Regno di Sicilia nell'Europa del Duecento: per una storia comparata delle codificazioni europee,* atti del convegno internazionale di studi per le celebrazioni dell'VIII Centenario della Nascita di Federico II, Messina, Reggio Calabria 1995.

RUFINO DI CONCORDIA, *Le benedizioni dei patriarchi,* trad. a cura di M. Veronese, Roma 1995.

E. VILLIERS, *Amuleti, talismani ed altre cose misteriose,* Milano 1995.

G. CALDARELLI, *Atti dei martiri,* Milano 1996.

G. CREMASCOLI, C. LEONARDI, *La Bibbia nel Medioevo,* Bologna 1996.

P. VENTURELLI, *Gioielli e gioiellieri milanesi. Storia, arte, moda (1450-1630),* Milano 1996.

A. MOTTANA, *Il libro sulle pietre di Teofrasto,* Trad. a cura di M. Napolitano, Testo presentato all'Accademia dei Lincei, Roma 1997.

R. LACHAUD, *Magia e iniziazione nell'Egitto dei faraoni. L'universo dei simboli e degli dei, spazio, tempo, magia e medicina,* trad. di Livia Pietrantoni, Roma 1997.

ILDEGARDA DI BINGEN, MARBODO DI RENNES, *Il libro delle Gemme,* trad. di Paolo Melis, Torino 1998.

M. G. LA GRUA, *Cristo nelle pietre preziose, per una rilettura biblica,* RnS, Palermo 1998.

G. V. SCHIAPPARELLI, *Scritti sulla storia della astronomia antica,* vol. 2, Milano 1998.

J. P. BRACH, *Il Simbolismo dei numeri,* a cura di P. L. Zoccatelli, trad. di R. Campagnari, Roma 1999.

P. BRAMBILLA BARCILON, P. C. MARANI, *Leonardo. L'Ultima Cena,* Milano 1999.

G. BUSI *Simboli del pensiero ebraico: lessico ragionato in settanta voci,* Torino 1999.

L. CASTELFRANCHI, C. PIGLIONE, F. TASSO, *Arti minori,* Milano 2000.

F. DI GIOVAMBATTISTA, *Il Giorno dell'espiazione nella Lettera agli Ebrei,* Roma 2000.

D. A. BROWN, *Quando l'Ultima Cena era nuova,* in *Il genio e le passioni, Leonardo e il Cenacolo. Precedenti, innovazioni, riflessi di un capolavoro,* a cura di P. C. Marani, Milano 2001.

D. CALCAGNO, *Il Sacro catino, specchio dell'identità genovese,* in *Xenia antiqua,* Roma 2001.

E. MILANO, P. DI PIETRO LOMBARDI, M. RICCI, A. M. VENTURI BARBOLINI, BIBLIOTECA ESTENSE, *Legenda aurea. Iconografia religiosa nelle miniature estensi,* Modena 2001.

S. GENTILE, C. GILLY, *Marsilio Ficino e il ritorno di Ermete Trismegisto,* Firenze 2001.

C. SCARPATI, *Leonardo scrittore,* Milano 2001.

A. ARTIOLI, *Il Cenacolo di Leonardo, Storia, significati, restauri,* in *Il restauro,* Soprintendenza per i beni architettonici e per il paesaggio di Milano, Milano 2002.

M. CICCUTO, *Figure d'artista. La nascita delle immagini alle origini della letteratura,* Fiesole 2002.

M. MANTOVANI, *Meditazioni sull'albero della Cabala,* Milano 2002.

A. SCHIMMEL, in *L'Uomo e i Simboli,* Milano 2002.

A. M. TRIPPUTI, *PGR, Per grazia ricevuta,* vol. 1, Bari 2002.

C. VASOLI, *Le filosofie del Rinascimento,* a cura di P. C. Pissavino, Milano 2002.

P. VENTURELLI, *Leonardo da Vinci e le arti preziose: Milano tra XV e XVI secolo,* Venezia 2002.

N. SALA, G. CAPPELLATO, *Viaggio matematico nell'arte e nell'architettura,* Milano 2003.

W. R. LETHABY, *Architettura misticismo e mito,* a cura di G. Bilancioni, Bologna 2003.

S. LUCCHESI, *Archeogemmologia: le pietre nella Bibbia,* Testo della Conferenza, Torino 4 marzo 2003.

M. BINIECKA, *Gemme e oro: aspetti tecnologici, qualitativi, economici e sociali,* Consiglio nazionale delle ricerche, Roma 2004.

A. CARPIN, *Angeli e demòni nella sintesi patristica di Isidoro di Siviglia,* Bologna 2004.

M. J. KEMP, *Lezioni dell'occhio: Leonardo da Vinci discepolo dell'esperienza,* Milano 2004.

SEVERIANO DI GABALA, *In apostolos,* testo, traduzione, introduzione e note a cura di D. Righi, Roma 2004.

P. LIPPINI, *Furono i Domenicani a salvarlo dopo il bombardamento dell'agosto 1943,* in *L'Ultima Cena di Leonardo da Vinci. Una lettura storica, artistica e spirituale del grande capolavoro,* Comunità dei Padri Domenicani di Santa Maria delle Grazie, Milano s.d.

EUSEBIO DI CESAREA, Storia ecclesiastica, trad. a cura di F. Migliore e S. Borzì, Vol. 1, 2,23,7, Roma 2005.

S. CREMANTE, *Leonardo da Vinci. Artista, scienziato, inventore*, Firenze 2005.

H. LAMMER, M. Y. BOUDJADA, *Enigmi di pietra. I misteri degli edifici medievali*, trad. di A. Manco, Roma 2005.

M. ROSSI, *Disegno storico dell'arte lombarda*, Milano 2005.

G. T. Bagni, B. D'Amore, *Leonardo e la matematica*, Milano 2006.

F. CERVINI, C. SPANTIGATI, *Il tempo di Pio V, Pio V nel tempo: atti del Convegno internazionale di studi,* Bosco Marengo, Alessandria 2006.

E. SCHOONHOVEN, *Fra Dio e l'imperatore: il simbolismo delle pietre preziose nella Divina Commedia*, in Dante, *rivista internazionale di studi su Dante Alighieri*, Pisa – Roma 2006.

JACOPO DA VARAZZE, *Legenda Aurea*, traduzione a cura di G. P. Maggioni, Firenze 2007.

T. KATINIS, *Medicina e filosofia in Marsilio Ficino: il Consilio contro la pestilenza*, Istituto nazionale di studi sul Rinascimento, Roma 2007.

P. VEZZOSI, *E' lui il più bello: ritratti medicei nella villa-museo di Cerreto Guidi*, Firenze 2007.

G. B. LADNER, *Il simbolismo paleocristiano. Dio, cosmo, uomo*, Milano 2008.

S. MACIOCE, *Ori nell'arte: per una storia del potere segreto delle gemme*, Roma 2007.

S. MACRI', *Pietre viventi. I minerali nell'immaginario del mondo antico*, Torino 2009.

L. PACIOLI, *De divina Proportione*, a cura di A. Marinoni, Cinisello Balsamo (MI) 2010.

E. GALAVOTTI, L. ESPOSITO, *Cristianesimo primitivo. Dalle origini alla svolta costantiniana*, I edizione 2011.

J. T. LIENHARD, *Ministry*, Eugene, Oregon 2011.

K. PIETSCHMANN, *Liturgical Polyphony* and political ambition, in *Religion and the Senses* in *Early Modern Europe*, a cura di W. de Boer, C. Göttler, Leiden-Boston 2013.

E. SOLMI, *Vita segreta di un genio*, Roma 2013.

F. PIRO, *La tenda del deserto, architettura del primo santuario di Israele*, Lecce 2014.

F. CAROLI, *Leonardo. Studi di fisiognomica*, Milano 2015.

R. CONTE, *Epiphanius von Salamis, Uber die zwolf Steine im hohe- priesterlichen Brustschild (De duodecim gemmis rationalis): nach dem "Codex Vaticanus Borgianus*

Armenus" 31 (2014), in AA.VV., *Erga-Logoi,* Vol. 3, No. 2 (2015): *Rivista di Storia, Letteratura, Diritto e culture dell'antichità.*

S. GASBARRI, I busti del Pincio: *Nel Giardino della Memoria alla ricerca della nostra identità. Italia, caput mundi della cultura e della civiltà,* Roma 2016.

CCC (*Catechismo della Chiesa Cattolica – Catechism of the Catholic Curch*).

Web sites references:

http://ancient-hebrew.org/

www.bibbiaedu.it

biblegateway.com

it.cathopedia.org

laparola.net

mirabileweb.it

sangiudataddeo.net

santiebeati.it

santodelgiorno.it

treccani.it

w2.vatican.va

Biblical versions

Bibbia Sacra Vulgata (Vulgata)

CEI (Conferenza Episcopale Italiana)

ESVUK (English Standard Version UK)

NR 2006 (Nuova Riveduta 2006)

Photographic credits

- Dott. Ing. Tiziano Radice, photographer and videomaker, also with drone.

- Last Supper of lombard artist (attributed to Andrea Solario), ©Thill NV, Brussels, Belgium.

- Last Supper of Giampietrino (kind courtesy of Royal Academy of Arts, London).

- Ultima Cena di Marco da Oggiono, photo©RMN-Grand Palais (musée de la Renaissance, château d'Ecouen) / Gérard Blot

- Last Supper preserved in the Episcopal Seminary of Savona, Italy, (kind courtesy of Diocesi of Savona - copy authorization n. 04/16, date: 20.09.2016).

- Last Supper (attributed to Tommaso Aleni) preserved at the Monastry of San Sigismondo, Cremona, Italy (Authorization n° 207/16, date: 14.10.2016).

- Last Supper by Cesare da Sesto, preserved in the Church of Sant'Ambrogio, Ponte Capriasca, Ticino, Switzerland.

- Last Supper preserved in the Minoritenkirche, Wien (kind courtesy of Dr. Manfred Zips).

45440428R00071

Made in the USA
San Bernardino, CA
30 July 2019